REBECCA WINTERS

Harlequin Romance® presents you with this emotional new duet by Rebecca Winters. She's won many fans around the world with her wonderfully compelling, sparkling stories.

Welcome to:

TWIN BRIDES
Here come the grooms!

Callie and Ann may look the same, but when they jet off to Italy they meet two very different men—one's a gorgeous prince, the other an enigmatic tycoon!

Bride Fit for a Prince
March 2003 (#3739)

Rush to the Altar
April 2003 (#3743)

Don't miss this sensational duet brought to you by Harlequin Romance®.

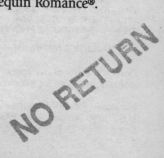

Rebecca Winters, an American writer and mother of four, was excited about the new millennium because it meant another new beginning. Having said goodbye to the classroom where she taught French and Spanish, she is now free to spend more time with her family, to travel and to write the Harlequin Romance® novels she loves so dearly.

Rebecca loves to hear from readers. If you wish to email her, please visit her website at: www.rebeccawinters-author.com

If you enjoyed Callie's story, don't miss her twin sister's search for her very own Mr. Right.

Look out for Ann's story, on sale next month in Harlequin Romance®!

Books by Rebecca Winters

HARLEQUIN ROMANCE®

3673—CLAIMING HIS BABY
3693—THE BRIDEGROOM'S VOW
3703—THE PRINCE'S CHOICE*
3710—THE BABY DILEMMA
3729—THE TYCOON'S PROPOSITION

*HIS MAJESTY'S MARRIAGE—2-in-1 with Lucy Gordon

BRIDE FIT FOR
A PRINCE
Rebecca Winters

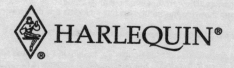

TORONTO • NEW YORK • LONDON
AMSTERDAM • PARIS • SYDNEY • HAMBURG
STOCKHOLM • ATHENS • TOKYO • MILAN • MADRID
PRAGUE • WARSAW • BUDAPEST • AUCKLAND

ISBN 0-373-03739-2

BRIDE FIT FOR A PRINCE

First North American Publication 2003.

Copyright © 2002 by Rebecca Winters.

Visit us at www.eHarlequin.com

Printed in U.S.A.

CHAPTER ONE

"CALLIE? Wait up!"

Callie Lassiter had just finished strapping her satchel to the back of her motorcycle when her twin came running up to her. They hadn't seen each other for five months at least. It was September already. Where had the time gone?

Her sister looked beautiful as always. As for Callie, she had mud all over her, even in her braided hair which no longer looked ash-blond. She smelled to high heaven.

"I better not hug you." Callie laughed.

"Please don't!" Ann laughed back, making no attempt to touch her.

"I thought you were in Los Angeles. Why didn't you let me know you were coming to Prunedale? I would have made arrangements to take a couple of days off."

"There wasn't time. Something happened last night I have to talk to you about, so I caught a plane to San Jose today."

"How did you know I was over here at the Oliveros'?"

"Dr. Wood said you'd ridden out this way earlier to help deliver a cow that was in trouble. I took a chance you might still be here."

The heifer had been in trouble all right, but no longer. The cute little baby calf was doing great and so was its mother.

"What's wrong?"

"My agent called me at midnight last night and told me I've been offered the big part in a new film with Cory Sievert that I auditioned for two weeks ago!"

"You're kidding! That's fantastic, Ann!" she cried, hugging her sister before she remembered not to.

Ann backed away, brushing herself off. "I couldn't believe it. The actress first chosen for the part has turned out to be pregnant. Yesterday she went to the hospital with kidney stones and is out of commission. They needed to cast another actress immediately. I was the lucky one!"

After all the bit parts, she realized this was the big break Ann had been living for all these years, but Callie also knew her sister very well. She could have phoned her with this kind of news. There was something her sister wanted, otherwise she wouldn't have flown up from L.A. without notice.

"I'm thrilled for you, Ann!"

"Me, too, but there's just one little problem. Last night I won another contest!"

"That's a problem? How much was the prize this time?"

Over the years her sister had entered more beauty contests than Callie could count. With those classic features and long legs, she'd won some considerable cash earnings, all part of Ann's plan to stay afloat while she gained publicity to become a Hollywood star.

"Something really incredible, but I can't follow through with it, not now that I have to report on the set first thing in the morning. This film is going to launch my career, Callie. That's why you have to help me out. I've got a favor to ask of you."

Uh-oh. "What did you win?"

"Let's just say I was picked for something."

Callie's expressive brows furrowed. "Picked for what?"

"First I have to explain, so please hear me out. About a month ago I signed up to participate in a Hollywood charity benefit for the homeless called Who Wants To Marry A Prince? I heard about it from some girls while we were auditioning for a role—"

"Wait a minute!" Callie stopped her cold. "You signed up for a benefit like that after you were in that other ghastly, humiliating benefit last year, Who Wants To Marry A Billionaire?"

"It was for the publicity," Ann defended. "Luckily I wasn't chosen on that one. But even if he'd picked me, I would have pretended to faint, then refused to get married. The runner-up would have been forced to marry that overweight, over-the-hill American billionaire at his hotel in Las Vegas.

"But this benefit was different! A gorgeous, wealthy European prince was coming all the way to Hollywood to choose the right bride for him. It sounded so romantic and smacked of the days of Prince Rainier of Monaco coming to America to claim the actress Grace Kelly for his bride."

"What it smacks of is a wolf in prince's clothing," Callie remarked in a scathing tone.

"How can you say that? The girls and I agreed that even if we didn't get chosen, it was for a worthy cause and would give us great publicity because we knew there'd be a lot of talent scouts and film directors in the audience. The exposure might help land us a big movie contract.

"You should have seen this prince, Callie. He was

wearing his royal outfit when he appeared onstage after I'd been chosen along with the other finalists. I have a picture of him. Here." She whipped out a photo Callie had no choice but to look at. "Isn't he incredible?"

Callie had to admit he resembled every little girl's idea of Prince Charming. Dark brown hair, warm brown eyes. Dimples.

"I almost fainted when he walked past all of us, then knelt in front of me. He whispered that he'd made his decision the moment he'd seen my picture on the application.

"Before I could blink, he slipped this amazing betrothal ring on my finger. Can you believe that out of all the beautiful women there, he chose *moi*?"

Actually Callie wasn't at all surprised. Ann was a raving beauty.

"So—have you informed him the wedding's off because you're too busy working on your next film?"

After a telling silence, "Not yet. That's what I wanted to talk to you about. You see, when my application was accepted for the benefit, the host was smart enough to put a clause in the contract I signed that wasn't in the Who Wants To Marry A Billionaire contract."

Callie's black-fringed eyes spit green sparks. "You mean you made the same mistake again and signed another contract *before* you paraded back and forth in front of the prince like a prize steer at a cattle auction?"

"Don't be so earthy, Callie. I'll have you know I was careful to read the small print. It made all the difference. That's why I signed papers in front of the attorney for the benefit, as well as the prince's private attorney."

Callie felt ill. "What did the special clause say?"

"You have to marry the prince within twenty-four

hours of your arrival in his country and live with him for one month. If at the end of that time either of you wants to back out of the marriage, you can get a divorce, no questions asked, and the homeless charity still get their money.

"It's a perfect setup. If you don't want to stay married, you'll have won a free trip to Europe and all the publicity that goes with it."

Her sister was taking a long time to get to the point. When Ann tossed her head back like that, it was the signal that she was really nervous about something.

"I suppose if you actually did fall in love with the prince and he fell in love with you, then you'd stay married and live happily ever after in his palace without having to worry about money again. But only if it's the life you really want, which I don't and never did!"

Callie groaned in horror. Her sister's one track mind had gotten her into some awful scrapes in the past, but nothing as bad as this. The heat of anger filled her cheeks.

"What does this prince do? Go around attempting to get married every few months in the name of charity because he can't have an intimate relationship with a woman any other way? What's wrong with him? He could be an ax murderer for all you know.

"Have you considered you could be walking into danger? What if you got pregnant?

"Do you honestly believe the prince would let that thirty day stipulation stand in the way if you were carrying a royal heir? If you think for one minute he'd consider divorcing you and allow you to leave the country with his child, then I know you've lost your mind!"

Ann's identical green eyes gleamed like a cat's.

"There's no chance of my getting pregnant. Trust me. But that's not the point. If you saw his pedigree, you wouldn't have all these misgivings."

"*Misgivings*—don't you know what he's done is without a doubt the most monstrous, awful, barbaric, ludicrous, absurd thing I've ever heard of? Annabelle Lassiter—how could you put so little value on yourself? Selling yourself off to the highest bidder just to get in the movies? Where's your pride?"

"Pride doesn't pay my rent," her sister retorted. "Naturally if I'd known my agent was going to call me last night with news that I'd landed the most coveted Hollywood film role of the year, I would never have gotten myself involved in the benefit in the first place and wouldn't be in this dilemma now."

"What dilemma? Tell the benefit committee you're going to be in a movie so they'll have to choose one of the other contestants for the prince."

"I already tried that, but it didn't work. This morning, before I flew up here, I asked my attorney to look over the contract I signed. He says there's no way I can get out of it. That's why you're the only person on the planet who can help me."

"Oh, no, you don't."

Callie didn't even want to think about it. She put on her helmet, then started up her motorcycle and rode down the country road toward the Pike's farm. Their calico cat, Baxter, had gone off his food. Callie had promised to take a look at him on her way back to the clinic.

Unfortunately Ann followed in her rental car. By the time Callie started to unfasten her helmet, her sister had caught up with her and thrust something in her face.

"Take another look at his picture. His name is Prince Enzo Tescotti. He's twenty-eight, only a year older than we are. You can see there's absolutely nothing wrong with him."

"I might have known he'd be an Italian," Callie muttered. "Oh, brother."

"Here are the first-class round trip airline tickets to Turin, Italy, where he and his royal cortege will be at the terminal to greet you after you get off the plane.

"You'll have to fly out of Los Angeles. Luckily you went to England for that vet conference after graduation, so you already have a passport. I've also purchased your round trip tickets from San Jose to L.A.

"Since your overseas flight leaves day after tomorrow, you'll have to fly to L.A. tomorrow. You can stay overnight at my apartment. I'll drive you to the airport the next morning on my way to the studio."

Callie shook her head. "Even if I were willing, which I'm not, I can't leave my work."

"That's all been taken care of. When I told Dr. Wood you'd won a month's vacation in Italy, all expenses paid, he was thrilled for you. He agreed you work too hard and are due a long vacation. I swear he told me he'd get along just fine until you came back. So you're set!"

"Just like that?" Callie snapped her fingers. "You're forgetting one thing. I'm not the one in this family who treats life like it's one big joke." She handed the tickets and picture back to her sister.

"Maybe that's because you take it far too seriously," Ann responded in a quiet voice. "I'm not like you. I hated the way Dad's death left us in debt. Mom scrimped and still ended up having to sell the farm. You're just like her."

"She did what was necessary to keep you and me alive!" Callie defended.

"Mom could have married several men who asked her, but she didn't."

"That's because she loved Daddy too much."

"So much that her life was miserable after that and she ended up dying of a heart attack. You'll probably die early, too, and I'll be left alone."

"*Ann—*"

"It's true. You work too hard and you've got years of vet school loans to pay off. You don't even have a car and are forced to ride around on a secondhand motorcycle."

"You know I've always had a thing for motorcycles." Hers happened to be a yellow and black *Danelli Strada 100 Sports Bike* that had won every competition for a decade before the company unexpectedly ceased to exist. "It still gets me where I need to go. Best of all, it's mine!" she said staring pointedly at Ann's rental car.

"But you live in a tiny two-room apartment at the back of the vet clinic where you can hear every sick animal in North Monterey county howling and meowing in your sleep.

"You have no love life and no hope of getting one working for Dr. Wood who's old enough to be our great grandfather. Most of the time you spend your life mucking out stalls or pig pens in order to get your job done! When was the last time you did something exciting or had any fun?"

"I have fun as a vet," Callie defended. "It's what I wanted from the first time Jasper almost died when we were nine years old and Dr. Wood cured him. In a few years I'll make a good enough living to be able to afford a place of my own. In the meantime, I'm not complaining and plan to live a long time. I happen to love the life I lead.''

"So do I! That's why I can't lose this opportunity now. This movie ensures I'll be able to live at least five years off the money they're going to pay me.''

"That's a lot of money,'' Callie said quietly. "I'm glad for you, and sorry you've gotten yourself into this mess.''

"Not as sorry as I am. I only wanted to be *seen,* not chosen.''

At this point Ann's eyes were brimming with tears. They were the genuine article. Callie looked away, unable to handle it when her sister got upset like this. It didn't happen very often.

"You should have thought of that sooner.''

"Do you know something? You've grown hard since veterinary school. I don't understand it.''

Had she?

Somewhere deep inside, Ann's comment hurt. Since their mother's death, Callie's emotions probably had closed off. She hadn't realized it showed.

"Whatever happened to my sister who once played tricks on all her would-be boyfriends and then used me to bail her out? As I recall, I never turned you down when you begged me to go out with them because you'd changed your mind. And I never told them that we'd switched places either.''

Callie had forgotten about those happier days. She had to admit Ann had been a real trouper way back in high school when Callie had developed this horrendous crush on their neighbor's son, Jerry. No other guy could compete.

"That's what I'm doing now, Callie. Begging you to help me. My agent told me I have to report for makeup at six in the morning. If I don't show up, not only will I be out of the film, I'll be blackballed and he'll drop me as a client. Where else do I go for help except my family? Please."

Feeling her last escape hole closing over her, Callie closed her eyes tightly. "You're asking a lot."

"I know. If it's any help, I've worked out a contingency plan."

"What is it?"

"I've written out a ten thousand dollar check to the prince. It's all the money I have in the world until I'm paid in two weeks. When you get to Italy, be honest with the prince.

"Tell him you're my sister, that you're there on my behalf. Explain that the same night I was in the benefit, I was offered the most important film role of my life.

"Hand him the betrothal ring and the check. It should cover the airline tickets and any other expenses he incurred. Tell him if he wants more money because I've broken the contract, he'll have to ask his attorney to contact my attorney through my agent.

"Once you've delivered my message and given him everything, you can turn around and come home on the next flight. I promise you he's a sweetheart. All the other finalists thought he was a darling and wished they'd been chosen. There won't be any problem with him."

"You don't know anything about his character," Callie muttered, feeling herself crumble because Ann's suggestion actually sounded plausible. She supposed that if she talked to the prince face-to-face, and offered him the money while she explained the situation...

"Maybe not, but I'm certain he's not the monster you've made him out to be. Just remember, Callie—I didn't sign up to be in that benefit with the intention of backing out if I'd been chosen. I would have gone through with it.

"But when my agent called with the news that I could replace that other actress, I couldn't turn it down. Look—you've already established your career. Couldn't you find it in your heart to take three days away from your routine to help me forge mine? Is it really too much to ask?"

When Ann put it like that...

"No," Callie conceded quietly. She did owe her sister for past favors.

"Oh, Callie—thank you, thank you." She broke down sobbing and threw her arms around her, mindless of the dirt.

"I'm sorry I gave you such a hard time," Callie murmured. "Three days isn't such a sacrifice. I'll suggest to the prince that he make arrangements to marry the runner-up. She had to sign that contract, too. My guess is she'll jump at the chance to take your place."

"I *know* she will!" Ann sniffed and let her go. "She's a beautiful brunette and is a graduate student in architecture from Carmel. They showed a film clip of her winning all these horseback riding competitions. I can't understand why the prince didn't pick her to begin with. She was much more suited to being a real princess."

Thank goodness there *had* been a runner-up. It would make Callie's task easier.

"Why don't you go back to the clinic and wait for me. I'm not sure how long I'll be at the Pike's."

"That's okay. I'll sit in the car and work on my lines

for tomorrow's shoot. When you're through, I'll follow you home and help you pack.''

''What's to pack? Aside from some extra underwear, a clean pair of jeans and a top should last me for the thirty-six-hour trip over and back. It's all the time I can spare. The Selanders's mare will be having her foal any day now. I plan to be here for it.''

''But you can't meet the prince dressed that casually—'' Ann cried out aghast.

''I'm not his betrothed. No one's going to care what the messenger looks like.''

Ann shook her head. ''I just hope you won't feel foolish when all these people are at the airport in full royal regalia.''

''He'll only get what he deserves for buying you like you were the goods at a slave market. The whole thing is so disgusting I still can't believe it.''

The prince might be attractive, but Callie would bet her life there was a strain of mental illness that ran in his royal family. As far as she was concerned, the sooner she got Ann out of this wretched situation, the better.

Two days later the commuter flight from Milan where Callie had gone through customs, taxied to a stop at the airport in Turin. *Torino* to the locals.

She unfastened her seat belt, anxious to meet the prince and get this over with. Though she was tired, traveling first-class had made it a pleasant enough experience. In an hour she'd be on the return flight and sleep all the way home.

Looping the strap of her tote bag over her shoulder, she followed the other passengers to the waiting area inside the terminal.

There were masses of people standing about. Callie braced herself for whatever fanfare awaited her, but to her surprise nothing happened. She walked around for a few minutes, expecting to be approached, or to hear her sister's name being called over the public address system at least.

How odd... It appeared no royal contingent had come to the airport for her yet. Maybe something unavoidable had occurred and the prince couldn't help being late.

Slowly the crowds thinned until everyone had gone except a dangerous-looking male in his mid-thirties with overly long black hair seated on one of the lounge chairs. He was reading an Italian newspaper. His well-worn jeans and black leather jacket emphasized a strong, powerful physique.

There was something about Italian men Callie had noticed from the moment she'd entered the Milan terminal. No matter what they wore, they had a certain style and elegance that caused them to stand out from other men.

She grudgingly admitted that's why they had the reputation for being seductive lovers. Especially this dark, arresting stranger whose aquiline features made her heart race for no good reason.

When he looked up suddenly and she met his jet-black gaze head on, heat enveloped her like a desert storm. She turned away, embarrassed to be caught staring like that. Without hesitation she headed for the terminal desk.

If the prince didn't come soon, she'd write a note of explanation and slip it in the envelope with the check and ring. Before she boarded the plane for her return flight home in half an hour, she would ask the airline employee to make certain it was put in the prince's hands.

"Signorina Lassiter?"

A deep, unfamiliar male voice spoke directly behind her. She spun around to discover the striking-looking stranger standing too close to her, robbing her of breath. He was a tall man, at least six feet two. At five feet eight, she noticed things like that.

His searching black eyes seemed to consume her features and hair which she wore in one fat braid halfway down her back.

"Are you from the palace?"

There was a pregnant pause. "That's right. My name is Nicco." He spoke excellent English with a heavy accent she found disturbingly appealing.

"I understood Prince Enzo was going to meet the plane."

"I'm afraid he was unavoidably detained. I was dispatched to...take care of you."

"Who are *you?* One of his bodyguards?"

His lips twitched. "Would it make you feel safer if I said yes?"

Not particularly. If the truth be known, Callie had already imagined this man could handle himself in any situation. What bothered her was his mocking arrogance which had caught her on the raw. It appeared the prince's emissary had kept her waiting on purpose.

He didn't like her.

She'd sensed that instinctively, yet she couldn't blame him. Any woman who would be a part of a benefit in order to sell her body to an unknown prince deserved the world's scorn.

On the other hand, any man who would work for a prince who had no morals was equally despicable.

"Let's just say that by answering my question with a

question, you've come off sounding positively Machiavellian. But then I shouldn't be surprised. You did say your name was *Niccolo*. The master of cunning. A throwback to your ancient ancestor perhaps?''

For a split second his eyes glittered with some unnamed emotion that sent a dart of fear coursing through her nervous system.

"The prince will be impressed with your knowledge of Italian political history, *signorina*. It seems there are depths to you yet to be plumbed. Shall we get your bags?''

"I didn't bring any.''

"Of course not,'' he murmured in a silky voice. "A princess-to-be must have an entirely new wardrobe from the skin out.'' He slid an index finger down her cheek. "Yours feels like velvet. No wonder Prince Enzo couldn't resist you.''

"Is that one of your jobs? To inspect the royal merchandise?'' she snapped to cover the shock wave that had just passed through her body.

"Call it a lapse I couldn't resist. It won't happen again. Now that you're his fiancée, the prince won't allow another man to touch you on pain of death.''

She flashed him an icy smile. "How feudal of your master to send you ahead to discover my fatal flaw. I'll warn you now. I have several of them.''

A sardonic gleam entered his eyes. "I hadn't thought to enjoy my mission this much. Except for the wedding dress which I understand was purchased some time ago, the prince told me to accommodate your every desire.

"As soon as we leave the airport, it will be my pleasure to take you shopping for your royal trousseau. Along the arcade of the Via Roma you will find our country's most fashionable couturier salons," he whispered in a husky tone, giving her voluptuous body a slow, frank appraisal.

Considering she was in jeans and a knit top that was several years old, the look he'd just given her was meant to be insulting. The sparring had gone on long enough.

"You won't be taking me any place because I have no need of a new wardrobe," she blurted with as much *hauteur* as she could summon.

"Then you truly are a dream come true, *signorina*. I will let the prince know you intend to keep him happy in the marriage bed for the entire thirty days and nights."

"Careful, Niccolo—your true colors are showing," she bit out as white-hot heat consumed her.

"If your lack of concern about clothes is one of the fatal flaws you were referring to, then I admit I'm looking forward to ferreting out the rest of them."

Anxious to wipe the gloating expression from his eyes she said, "Will you please give this to the prince for me?"

Callie reached in her bag that contained her toiletries along with a change of underwear, and handed him the velvet lined box. It held the betrothal ring. After opening the lid, he trapped her hand.

"Do you know this ring dates from the early sixteenth century when the House of Piemonte and the House of Monferrato formed a valuable alliance through marriage?"

To her shock he slid it on her ring finger. After studying it he said, "I wondered why you weren't wearing it. Now I have my answer.

"Though it's the most valuable of the collection in terms of the Tescotti family history, I can see how this heavy gold piece doesn't suit your delicate hand. I'll tell his highness to pick out something more modern from the family jewels."

At the moment, her hands were covered in a rash from washing and scrubbing them so much before surgery. She'd tried every cream in existence, but they still itched and had blotchy spots he rubbed several times. Callie pulled her hand away, shaken by his touch which had arced through her body like a current of electricity.

Pulling off the ring, she put it back in the box and shoved it at him. "I have something else you can give the prince." Once more she reached in her bag and handed him the envelope with the check inside.

He opened it. "Ten thousand dollars. To my knowledge, the prince had no expectations of a wedding present from you. However I'm aware of something he *would* like, and this is the exact amount to cover it." His eyes flashed black fire. "You're going to make him the happiest man alive."

Putting both items in his pockets, he cupped her elbow. "It's a beautiful fall afternoon. Since you don't require any clothes, I thought you might like a ride around the city to relax you. It's only fitting that you survey your kingdom before the wedding tomorrow. Shall we get started?"

Callie jerked her arm away. "I'm not going anywhere with you and that money *isn't* a wedding gift."

He stared at her through veiled eyes. "You're trembling. But surely there is no reason to be afraid of me. This close to the ceremony, I have sworn a sacred oath to protect you with my life. In fact I am the only person in the world who has Prince Enzo's complete trust.''

''Then you need to let him know there isn't going to be a wedding.''

His white smile was condescending. ''I thought only the groom had what you Americans call pre-wedding jitters. You are turning out to be a surprise in so many ways, I find myself utterly captivated.''

''Look, Nicco whoever-you-are—I'm going to be honest with you.''

''You mean you haven't been up to now?''

Callie forced herself to count to ten. ''I've been trying to tell you something. Before you jump to any more wrong conclusions, you need to hear me out. I'm *not* the woman his highness picked to marry.''

The amusement in his eyes maddened her. He pulled a photograph out of his back pocket. ''Then who is this?''

The picture he held up was obviously the photograph Ann had sent in with the application.

Smothering a groan she said, ''I know it looks like me. That's because I'm Ann's twin sister, Callie.''

''Callie.'' He mouthed her name. In the next breath he'd relieved her of her shoulder bag and pulled out her passport. He opened it and placed the picture next to the passport photo. ''According to this, your name is Callie *Ann* Lassiter.''

''Yes, I know. My sister is named Annabelle, but she goes by Ann. Our father wanted both of us to have our mother's name.''

His lips twitched. ''That's quite a lie you've dreamed up. Obviously you're frightened of this step you're about to take. For an aspiring Hollywood actress, who would have guessed it?''

She'd had enough of his barely veiled mockery. Taking a deep breath she said, ''You mistake my fright for frustration. It's because you won't listen to me. I'm going to try this one more time. I'm *not* the prince's intended!''

As if it were his divine right, he unsnapped the strap of her wallet and looked at her driver's license.

''Callie *Ann* Lassiter,'' he read her name aloud again.

She gritted her teeth. ''This isn't getting us anywhere. I flew over to explain to the prince that she can't marry him because she's starring in a new movie. The ten thousand dollars is to pay for the airline tickets and other expenses the prince incurred by choosing to be the celebrity for the benefit.''

When he didn't say anything, she went on with her explanation.

''She's very sorry about breaking the contract. I assure you she would have followed through with the marriage. But on the night of the benefit, her agent called with the opportunity of a lifetime. She couldn't pass it up.''

His continued silence infuriated her.

''They started filming in Hollywood yesterday and she had to be on the set at six in the morning. So she came to see me the day before yesterday and asked me if I would return the ring to the prince in person and give him the money.''

Callie wondered if he was even listening to her.

''If it's not enough, tell him to contact her agent who will confer with her attorney. She wrote his name and number on a piece of paper in the envelope. I think that's everything, and now I have to go. They're calling for my flight to Milan.''

Crowds had gathered once more, filling the terminal with noisy chatter.

''If I could have my wallet and passport please.''

To her great relief, he put everything in her bag and handed it to her with an enigmatic expression on his face. ''I will convey your message to the prince.''

Finally a reaction!

''Thank you. Please tell him I'm very sorry my sister didn't know about the movie offer in time to pull out of the benefit. But if he's as wonderful as my sister says he is, then I'm sure he'll have no problem finding another fiancée.

''Ann told me the first runner-up in the competition was dying to be picked. Remind the prince that she was the ravishing brunette who's also an expert equestrian. Oh, yes, and a graduate student in architecture. She'll make the right bride for his highness.

''If he acts right away, a private jet could be sent for her in time to arrive for tomorrow's ceremony. Now I really have to go. Goodbye.''

CHAPTER TWO

RELIEVED to get away from him, Callie handed her boarding pass to the airline person at the gate and hurried through the door to the plane. Once she'd found her seat and strapped herself in, she could finally relax.

The whole thing had gone much better than she'd hoped. In a way she was glad she hadn't been forced to deal with the prince. No matter how repulsed she was by his evil method to get himself a bride, it still would have been hard to look him in the eye and tell him her sister didn't want to marry him after all.

As for *Niccolo Machiavelli*, she needed to put him out of her mind and forget such a man existed. He'd excited her in a frightening kind of way, probably because he was foreign and an unknown quantity. Her body still tingled from the caress of his fingers on her cheek and hands.

She'd never reacted to a man's touch like that before. Worse, she felt a sense of loss she couldn't account for to realize she wouldn't be seeing him again.

It was very strange considering that lately Callie had decided maybe she and Ann had been born without a woman's normal feelings. All of their friends had found a husband by now. Many of them already had children.

Growing up, Callie and Ann had never suffered from a lack of dates. If anything, it had been the other way around. Yet neither of them had ever had a serious boyfriend.

At college and vet school there'd been quite a few students interested in her, but she'd been too absorbed in her studies to get involved. It was the same way for Ann who'd had dates with some well known actors. Yet her hope of being an actress was stronger than her desire to settle down.

Now, suddenly, a dark stranger had made Callie aware of herself as a flesh and blood woman with needs that must have been lying dormant all these years. How ironic to think it took an Italian male to wake her up to her own sensuality.

Not just any Italian man, Callie.

Her instincts about animals and people were usually right on. The man who worked for Prince Enzo was a breed apart from other men. She'd sensed it from the first moment she'd seen him sitting there in all his splendid indifference to the world around him.

Deep inside she had the disquieting feeling he was going to be unforgettable. The thought was so alarming, she reached for her novel in a desperate attempt to get her mind on anything else besides him.

Little by little the seats filled. She tried to concentrate on the story, but it was impossible. The plane couldn't take off fast enough to suit her.

A new flight attendant came on board. She smiled and chatted with each passenger. When she came to Callie she said, "Signorina Lassiter? If you would come with me, please."

Callie blinked. "Why? What's wrong?"

"I don't know. There are two policemen waiting inside the terminal to talk to you."

Oh, no. Nicco must have already reported to the

prince and now she was about to be detained. She should have known this was too easy.

"As a matter of courtesy to you, I told them I would find you. I'm sure you don't want to be embarrassed by having them come on board for an interrogation."

"No, of course not—but the plane's about ready to take off."

"They said this shouldn't take long."

"I see. Thank you."

With growing trepidation she got up from the seat, grabbed her bag and followed the flight attendant into the terminal. Sure enough two Italian policemen in uniform were waiting for her at the exit.

"Signorina Lassiter?" The one with the moustache spoke first.

"Yes?"

"Signorina Ann Lassiter?" the other one questioned.

"No," she answered honestly. "My name is Callie. Ann is my sister."

"Your passport, please."

Once again she found herself opening her shoulder bag to get it out. The policeman took it from her and studied the picture.

"Thank you very much." He put it in his pocket. "If you'll come with us please."

"What do you mean? I have a plane to catch!"

The two officers smiled at each other before the one with the moustache said, "His royal highness learned that his beautiful American fiancée has prewedding nerves, a problem he finds extremely charming. He hopes that by now you have gotten over them enough to let us take you to him."

"No—" she cried out. "I mean, you don't understand—I'm *not* his fiancée! I can prove it if you'll just let me make one phone call!''

They broke into laughter. "He warned us you would put up a struggle. Come, *signorina*. No one keeps the prince waiting. However for his bride-to-be, he has made an exception this one time. We will take you to him.''

Callie sensed that if she continued to fight them, it would no longer be a joking matter. So much for her sister's belief that ten thousand dollars would settle everything.

I promise he's a sweetheart. All the other finalists thought he was a darling and wished they'd been chosen. There won't be any problem with him.

She'd known there'd been a catch somewhere. Now she thought she'd figured out what it was. *Prince Enzo held a title and nothing else!* That's why no royal contingent had been sent to greet her when she got off the plane and that's why he needed to buy a bride.

It was probably the reason he'd used his celebrity status to be the focus of a huge Hollywood benefit. No doubt he needed a wife to support *him!* Where else in the world but America would people pay big money for charity to rub shoulders with a European prince?

What better woman for him to pick than a shallow Hollywood actress with stars in her eyes for a brain, and a bank account that could feed all the homeless at once?

His choice of bride-to-be was beginning to make a lot of sense. Everyone knew a film idol was worth millions. Enough to keep him in the manner to which he'd been accustomed before his fortune had run out or he'd squandered it.

Apparently the prince's mouthpiece Nicco had wasted no time informing him that Signorina Lassiter had tried to back out of that damnable contract by insisting she was the wrong woman. He'd probably advised the prince to extort as much money from her as he could.

It looked as if Callie had no choice now but to meet his royal wretchedness himself, and set him straight about the farcical situation he'd brought on due to his own greed.

Once she could prove he was a has-been with nothing to show for it but an empty title, no court of law on either side of the Atlantic would require Callie's sister to hold up her end of that absurd contract. Talk about flawed…

In order not to make a scene, Callie allowed herself to be escorted by the two policemen. They entered a nearby elevator and descended to the next floor.

To her chagrin, thoughts of the prince's black-haired, slick-tongued envoy prevented her from concentrating fully over the impending confrontation. Undoubtedly Nicco had orchestrated the entire plot for the prince with the latter's promise of a healthy cut of Ann's film profits down the road.

Callie had been right all along. Nicco had Machiavellian blood running through his veins. Little did he know she had the fierce blood of her Norse ancestry running through hers…

When the elevator reached ground level, Callie's clover-green eyes narrowed as she prepared to do battle.

The police directed her to a door down the corridor which they unlocked. It opened onto the tarmac where their police van awaited. They helped her into the back where she sat on a bench. There were no windows to see out.

After being shut in, she had to endure a twenty-minute

drive without knowing where on earth they were taking her. Finally she felt the van slow down and come to a stop.

When they opened the doors to let her out, she discovered they'd driven to the rear of a medium-size apartment building somewhere in the heart of Torino.

In one of the nearby covered parking stalls she caught sight of a helmeted man getting off a motorcycle. Her eyes widened to discover it was a brand-new Danelli! That wasn't possible unless...

But when had the company started manufacturing them again?

To her shock, one of the police officers walked over to the driver of the fire-engine-red racing bike and handed him her passport. After a short conversation, he returned to the van. It backed out of the alley, leaving her standing there in a daze.

So *this* was the prince.

It appeared he had a little more money than she'd thought. Unless he was in debt up to his eyeballs and hoping his benefit bride would bail him out. To own such a fabulous machine would have set him back at least a hundred thousand dollars, maybe much more.

The man removed his helmet without bothering to smooth his black hair which had become disheveled.

"Buongiorno, signorina."

At the sound of the deep, seductive male voice she'd heard before, she let out a shocked gasp.

Nicco!

She hated it that he looked even more attractive than ever.

"Don't tell me—" she spoke first, anxious to quell the frantic beating of her heart. "I presume this is where the prince lives because he lost all his land and properties a long time ago.''

''How very astute of you.''

Callie ignored his sarcasm. ''I thought so. Thank you for being honest with me about that anyway. It's too bad my sister's not a famous, fabulously wealthy Hollywood actress yet. This whole thing might have had a different ending if she'd been ready to turn her back on the limelight and devote herself to a down-and-out prince.''

He gave a careless, elegant shrug of his broad shoulders. ''You can't blame a man for trying.''

''I suppose not. Unfortunately he risked everything on the wrong woman. But as she's my sister, I can vouch for her. Ann may be a little foolish at times, but she's a totally nice person who wants to make up to the prince for what has happened.

''After having met him, it's her belief he's a charming, civilized man who will understand the circumstances and be willing to work out any further financial arrangements with her attorney. I hope that's true so this thing can be cleared up right away. I have to fly home to the States tonight.''

''Let's go inside and find out, shall we?''

He led her through a back entrance and up a half flight of stairs to the second floor. Two doors down on the left he stopped and put a key in the lock. She heard barking.

''*Basta*, Valentino!''

The second the door opened, a gorgeous fawn-colored male boxer dog greeted him with such joy, it warmed Callie's heart. The first real smile she'd seen lit Nicco's eyes as he put his helmet on the foyer table and played around with the dog.

He spoke to it in Italian. She could just make out the

words Signorina Lassiter before he turned his head toward Callie. "The dog will give you five if you'll put out your hand."

"Give you five" was slang for two people slapping their palms together. Nicco's command of English was excellent. Obviously the prince had hired a modern-day Renaissance man to act for him at times like this.

She lifted her palm in the air. Valentino raised his paw and slapped hers with the right degree of strength so he didn't knock her down. Enchanted, she bent over and hugged him around the neck, scratching the sensitive spot behind his pointed ears.

"Oh, you're beautiful!" she cried softly.

For a reward he licked her mouth.

Callie burst into laughter. "I love you, too." She kissed his face. "Yes I do, you magnificent creature." Unable to help herself, she got down on her knees to inspect his white stocking feet. He had perfect coloring.

"You have the markings and bearing of a true champion." She kissed the top of his head one more time before standing up.

"For a dog and a human who don't understand each other's language, the two of you have managed to cross that boundary without problem," her host muttered in a dry tone.

The boxer walked around her, sniffing and licking her legs and hands. He could detect the scent of the vet hospital where she lived and worked.

"That's because I'm crazy about animals. How long has the prince had him?"

"Eight years now."

"The lucky man. Does he let you take Valentino for walks?"

"All the time."

"If I worked for him, that would be my favorite perk."

He flashed her a glance she couldn't decipher. "Come into the other room."

Anxious to meet the prince and get this over with, she followed Nicco's tall, rock-hard physique through a doorway to the living room of the apartment.

It was modestly furnished in what appeared to be secondhand furniture, exactly like the decor of her one bedroom apartment behind the clinic.

"Prince Enzo really has fallen on hard times. I feel right at home."

"He'll be glad to hear it," Nicco replied with a hint of mockery. "Please make yourself comfortable."

She sat down on one of the chairs. Valentino curled up at her feet. A few minutes of silence passed before she was prompted to ask, "What's taking the prince so long?"

"He's out for the moment."

When the meaning of his words sank in, her head reared. "What's going on here?"

Nicco sat down on the couch opposite her. "With his wedding day tomorrow, the prince is a busy man. He'll be along shortly."

"The prince better hurry if he expects the runner-up to arrive here in time."

He lounged back against the cushion, extending his long, powerful legs in front of him. "Come now, *signorina*. Surely you're not still maintaining that fictitious nonsense about a twin?"

Callie was on her feet in an instant. Her action disturbed the dog who instinctively tried to herd her so she wouldn't move from the room. Under normal circumstances she would have laughed at the endearing trait, but this situation was not amusing.

"Where's the phone? I'll get Ann on the line and she'll explain everything."

"I'm afraid the prince only uses a cell phone."

She took a struggling breath. "Then I assume you have one, too. May I use yours, please?"

"I would offer mine, but it needs to be recharged."

"How convenient."

As if proclaiming his innocence, he lifted those broad masculine shoulders still covered by his black Italian leather jacket. Her sarcasm had been utterly wasted on him.

"Before Prince Enzo arrives, we might as well begin a discussion of tomorrow's schedule. It's my job to prepare you for your nuptials. Why don't you sit down again and relax. Too much anxiety before the wedding ceremony will carry over into the bridal chamber.

"Ever since he saw your photograph last month, the prince has been anticipating your wedding night. He expects to find his new consort as eager as he is to begin your life together as husband and wife. It's up to me to make certain he isn't disappointed."

By now Callie's face was on fire. "And of course I don't have any say in the situation."

"None. Of your own freewill—in front of the attorney for the benefit as well Prince Enzo's personal attorney— you signed a contract I drew up for the prince myself. It is airtight, *signorina*. No power on earth, not even the Pope himself, can break it."

"*I* didn't sign it," she said calmly. "My sister did."

His gaze captured hers. She fought not to look away.

"Supposing that's true..." His voice trailed. "And you really do have an identical twin named Ann...it still won't stop the wedding from taking place tomorrow."

Something menacing in his tone sent a spiral of fear snaking through her body.

"If your sister had looked carefully at the profile given her on Prince Enzo by the benefit committee, she would have seen that the blood of the Borgia's as well as the Tescotti's runs through his veins.

"It's an historical fact that it was Cesare Borgia whom Machiavelli used as the model for his book about the prince who ruled without moral consideration for his terrified subjects."

He leaned forward. "If I were you, I'd start thinking very hard how you're going to influence your new husband *not* to have your sister arrested for sending you in her place. Prison is no place for the fiancée of Prince Enzo."

Callie refused to be intimidated. "Ann's not here to arrest."

"That's true. But you *are*..." His eyes had narrowed to black slits, like the kind you saw hollowed out in a castle turret where the bowmen shot their arrows.

"I thought Prince Enzo wanted me for his bride."

"*Naturalmente* you'll become his princess. When you've served your purpose, then you'll be placed under house arrest."

She felt her escape route closing fast, but she wasn't about to let him know that.

"So now we get down to the real reason for this absurd farce. My sister has already written him a check for ten thousand dollars which is all of her savings.

"With this next film, I'm sure she'll be able to give

him five times that amount. What's his price? If she can't meet it all the way, I'll go to my bank and see how much of a loan I can take out.'' At this rate Callie would be in debt for the rest of her life.

''Your loyalty to your sister is nothing short of astounding, *signorina*. That is if you *have* a sister,'' he drawled unnervingly. ''It's a pity money is not the consideration here.''

He reached in his pocket and threw the check down on the coffee table for her to take back.

''Then what *is?*'' she blurted in exasperation. ''Why has he gone to all the trouble of choosing an American bride? Unless—''

She darted him a wicked smile. ''Unless, of course, he has some genetic defect handed down from the Borgias that every Italian woman of royal blood already knows about and has avoided like the bubonic plague.''

With the stealth of a panther, Nicco rose to his full height, bigger than life. ''You're not as empty-headed as I had supposed, so I'm not going to ruin the surprise. Tomorrow morning you'll find out for yourself just exactly what you, or your sister, agreed to marry.''

''That's barbaric!''

The moment she shouted the words, the boxer growled deep in his throat and went into his guard dog stance.

A taunting smile broke the corner of Nicco's hard mouth. ''Valentino likes you very much, which is surprising when you consider his passionate devotion to the prince. Keep your voice well modulated and he won't treat you as an intruder. It's the last thing he wants to do. As you can see, his short tail is wagging.''

Valentino she could handle. The dog was wonderful. As for Nicco, he'd backed her into a corner.

Letting go of the breath she'd been holding she said, "You had me brought to this apartment under false pretenses. I won't be seeing the prince until the wedding, will I."

"Now you're catching on, as you Americans are fond of saying."

He must have spent a lot of time around someone from the States. *How she'd love to wipe that triumphant expression from his good-looking face.*

There was no way she would be a victim if she could help it. An idea for escape had just come to her. If it didn't work, then she'd try something else.

"Since you leave me with no choice but to surrender, how about granting this condemned prisoner one last favor before her *execution* tomorrow?"

His white smile was so unexpected and electrifying, her heart almost jumped out of her body. "Short of asking for a reprieve, your wish is my command, *signorina.*"

"You mean that?" She infused a little trembling into her question to reveal a deceptive combination of fear and humility.

"Try me and find out."

"Could we go on that ride around the city you promised me earlier?"

"Of course. I'll arrange for the limousine."

"No—I mean on your motorcycle."

A strange quiet filled the room. It pleased her that her request was the last thing he'd expected to be asked.

"In a movie I once rented, this American woman rode on the back of this guy's motorcycle while they toured

Naples. It looked so fun the way he maneuvered them through the narrow streets and alleys. They were able to go exciting places a car wouldn't fit.''

He rubbed his jaw absently. ''Torino's a northern city of long parkways, gardens, promenades and right angles, *signorina*.''

Before she averted her eyes, she purposely let out a deep sigh he couldn't help hearing.

''It's all right, Nicco. I understand. Really I do,'' she said in the way she might speak to a small child.

After a suspicious pause, ''What is it you *think* you understand?''

Good. She'd piqued his curiosity, just as she'd hoped.

''That your responsibility is to protect me until tomorrow.''

''And?'' he bit out impatiently. When she looked at him again, his eyes glittered with an unfathomable light.

''I should have realized you don't feel confident enough to show me the sights on your bike without having an accident. You could have just told me the truth, but I forgot your pride. I understand the Italian male's is more inflated than that of the other men of the world.''

He had no idea how much satisfaction it gave her to say that to him.

A sardonic smile broke out on his lips. ''If anything, I was trying to protect your female sensibilities. You would have to cling to me like you were my second skin,'' he said in a husky tone, leaving her in no doubt what he was thinking.

''However if that's your heart's desire, far be it from me to deny Prince Enzo's lovely fiancée her final request.''

Again she looked away, thrilled to realize she'd accomplished her first objective. But she wasn't going to fool herself that obtaining her second goal would be as easy to achieve.

"The bathroom is down that hallway on the right. Feel free to freshen up while I find his helmet for you to wear."

She made a show of frowning. "But in the movie, the woman didn't wea—"

"Forget the film." He broke in without hesitation. "If, God forbid, something unforeseen should happen while we're out riding, *I* would never forgive myself if you suffered an injury. Prince or no prince."

He stood there with his hands on his hips, his appeal so virile and potent, her body trembled when she thought of being plastered against him.

"If you've changed your mind, *signorina*…"

Now he was baiting *her,* expecting *her* to back down.

"No. I'll be ready in a moment."

"That's good. We have very little daylight left."

She headed for the hallway on unsteady legs. That was the effect he had on her.

Valentino followed. She knew he was standing guard outside the bathroom door because she could hear him snoring. He sounded just like her own dog, reminding her how much she missed Chloe.

When she was ready and reached the foyer, Nicco was waiting for her with a helmet under his arm, another black one in his hand.

He rapped out something in Italian to the boxer who immediately took a sitting position. Then he opened the door.

"After you," he said to Callie, indicating she should exit first. She retraced their steps to the outside of the apartment building. By the time she approached his cycle, he'd already put on his helmet.

Up close she could read the name of the model. It was called a Danelli NT-1 super bike.

"How much does something like this cost?"

"In lira or dollars?" he drawled.

"Dollars."

"Upward of $150,000 or more."

Even more than she'd thought. "For a down-and-out prince, he must pay you a hefty salary to afford this."

Ignoring her comment, he lowered the other helmet over her head and fastened the chin strap. His piercing black eyes trapped hers briefly before he moved to drop the rear foot pegs.

While she stood there in a daze, he threw his leg over the seat and straddled his bike. Once he'd started the powerful engine, he turned toward her.

"When you get on, place your feet on the pegs and wrap your arms around my waist, interlocking your fingers. That's all you have to do." He lowered his shield and waited.

From the second she'd laid eyes on Nicco, she'd known he was a dangerous man. Never in her wildest dreams did she imagine she'd get anywhere near a motorcycle like his, let alone ride on one. She bet it could reach over a hundred miles per hour in less than ten seconds. To feel that kind of lightning acceleration was going to be thrilling.

Heavens—if it weren't for the ghastly trouble Ann had gotten herself into, Callie would be having the time of her life.

Her heart pounded outrageously as she watched him

pull in the clutch and put the bike in gear. He was impatient to go, letting her know it was now or never.

With an eagerness she couldn't suppress, she jumped on behind him and adjusted her shoulder bag.

"I'm ready," she said, placing her sneaker-clad feet on the pegs. With a tug on her face shield, she lay against him and slid her arms around his hard-muscled body. No sooner had she intertwined her fingers than the bike sprang to life as if it had a will of its own.

He maneuvered them down the alley to the street. Then there was an initial leap and everything became a blur. They literally flew along the parkway to join the freeway.

CHAPTER THREE

THIS was ecstasy.

Nicco had incredible control as he wove so smoothly between cars. The daring way he took corners with breathtaking accuracy, every practiced move as she leaned with him, conveyed the expertise of a racing pro.

When he wasn't working for the prince, did he race? Was that how he could afford the bike? Or was this a special model paid for by sponsors?

A rush of adrenaline surged through her veins at the possibility she could be riding with one of the very best in the world. Yet she sensed he was still being careful to make certain nothing happened to her.

Callie wondered where he was taking them. The freeway seemed to be leading away from Torino's core to the outskirts. They whizzed past centuries-old residences and fairy-tale palaces of Baroque design.

By the time the sun dipped below the horizon, Torino with its four rivers and miles of gardens had been left behind. They'd reached an alpine valley that looked like a patchwork quilt of vineyards. A marvelous fruity essence seemed to envelop them.

Though the air had grown cooler, Nicco's warmth had invaded her body from her shoulders down. They were melded like two hot metals in a refiner's fire. The feeling of oneness was indescribable.

Never wanting their magical ride to end, she moaned in disappointment when he pulled off the road to follow a path through the vegetation. It was evident he knew about this spot. She assumed he wanted to rest for a minute before returning to the city.

Soon they arrived at a charming three-story farmhouse with a portico. Closed green shutters stood out against the pale orange exterior.

He geared down and came to a stop in the empty courtyard. The place appeared deserted to her. Remembering her plan, *now* would be the best time to make her getaway. Otherwise she might never have another opportunity.

Callie quickly got down from the bike and lifted the shield of her helmet. While she waited for him to climb off, she looked all around. Tall cypress trees were silhouetted against the sky, heralding the approach of night. She would need the motorcycle's headlights to help her find the way out of the mountains.

The second he swung his leg over she said, "That was an exhilarating ride. Before we go back to town, can I sit on it by myself for a minute?"

Nicco was still wearing his helmet which made it impossible to read his expression. He raised his shield.

"Go ahead."

"Do you think you could help me up?"

He made a little sound which could have been exasperation. She wasn't sure, but he did as she asked. With effortless masculine economy he lifted her on to the seat which she straddled.

"This is more exciting than opening my favorite present on Christmas morning! How do you make the dials light up like an airplane cockpit?"

With a swift movement he reached in front of her to turn on the key which was still in the ignition. The motion caused his arm to brush against her chest. Such intimate contact, even if it was accidental, sent her pulse zinging off the charts.

"I-it's a beautiful work of art isn't it?" her voice almost squeaked because she was shaking so hard in reaction.

"Are we still talking about the bike?" he asked in a sensuous tone.

The darkness hid the red staining her cheeks.

To her surprise his hands went to his chin strap. He was about to remove his helmet. She couldn't understand why, not when she assumed they'd be going right back to the city. Still, it was the exact kind of distraction Callie could take advantage of to carry out her next move.

She waited till he started to lift it over his head. Wasting no more time, she kicked the stand back, then pushed the start button. As she pulled in the clutch at the same time, the bike took off like a missile shot from a silo.

Callie heard an immediate explosion of Italian invective behind her, but it quickly faded because of the engine's whine. Praying to gain as much time as possible, she opened up on the dirt road.

Good heavens—there was so much power between her legs, she almost lost control as it ate up the kilometers leading down the main road to Torino.

If she could reach the American Embassy, she would ask for help getting home. At that point Nicco could claim his motorcycle while Callie's sister arranged for an attorney to deal with Prince Enzo.

Five miles later she whipped through the tiny town of Monferrato. About a mile beyond it, the bike seemed to lose steam. She downshifted and gave it more throttle. Nothing happened.

To her horror, the fuel gauge registered empty!

No-o-o-o-o-o.

She had no choice but to coast to the side of the road and pull to a stop.

Much as she wanted to thumb a ride from a passing car, she didn't dare leave a $150,000 bike sitting out in the open. It was too heavy to push anywhere, so the only thing she could do was wait until a motorist came along and she could pay for them to buy her a can of gas back in Monferrato.

Someone must have been watching out for her because she saw an old blue truck coming along the road in her direction. The driver slowed down and pulled over to the shoulder. Leaving the headlights on, he got out of the cab.

As she watched, she saw a tall, well-honed male walk toward her carrying a gas can in one hand, a helmet in the other. When she realized who it was, her legs began to tremble and wouldn't stop.

Looking at him or touching him, she couldn't deny Nicco was an exceptionally beautiful man.

In the animal kingdom there were gradations of beauty. Valentino took top honors for a boxer dog. If there were such a contest for the human male, Nicco would be hailed as grand champion. To find herself this attracted to him made it particularly hard to remember he was her enemy.

Finding her had been child's play to Nicco who'd known his bike was almost out of gas.

The reason he'd picked that particular farmhouse to visit was no longer a mystery. Evidently it belonged to a friend who was happy to do any favor for him, even providing him with gas or lending him a truck.

"I underestimated you, *signorina,*" came his deep, chilling voice before he put on his helmet. "Believe me, it won't happen again."

The contempt in those black eyes sweeping over her was surprisingly hurtful.

"You can't blame a girl for trying," she mocked his earlier words through the open shield of her helmet. But when she tried to shrug her shoulders the way she'd seen him do, her effort failed miserably in the translation.

Ignoring her, he moved to his bike and unlocked the lid to the gas tank. At this point she was shivering from the cold as well as nerves while she waited for him to fill it.

Once that was accomplished, he tossed the can into the roadside vegetation. Then he did something unexpected and removed his jacket.

"Put this on." He held it out to her.

She shook her head. "That's all right. I don't need it."

"Prince Enzo will never forgive me if you should come down with a bad cold on your wedding day. So you will wear it, even if I have to bundle you into it myself."

There was no mistaking his intent if she refused him, so she slipped it on and zipped up the front over her purse which hung from her neck. But she would never give him the satisfaction of knowing how good it felt to be enveloped in the heavy, Kevlar-reinforced leather where his body warmth was still trapped.

"Get on the bike, *signorina.*" There was steel in his demand.

She climbed behind him and once again wrapped her arms around his rock-solid frame. The heat from his skin crept through the thickness of his turtleneck to her hands and fingers interlocked against the muscles of his taut stomach.

With a nudge of his boot, the kickstand went back.

"What about the truck?" she cried.

"It's a little late for you to be showing concern for someone else's property."

His withering comment only added to the guilt she was feeling for having done anything as outrageous as stealing his fabulous bike almost out from under him in order to escape.

He maneuvered it around so they were facing the other way. Like déjà vu it surged forward, carrying them toward Monferrato with dizzying speed. This time she noticed he gave no thought to the passenger clinging to him.

Now that he had proof she could ride, he let his bike fly as much from the sheer enjoyment of the rush it gave him, as from the anger fueling his emotions. Having pulled this unforgivable stunt, she knew he wouldn't give her the slightest chance to get away from him again.

Since he'd denied her the use of a telephone to call for outside help, she would have to come up with something more ingenious. They were at war and it was a prisoner's duty to try to escape.

Callie couldn't possibly marry Prince Enzo.

She wouldn't!

In a few minutes she heard him say, "After you, *signorina*."

Nicco opened the door of the farmhouse they'd driven

to earlier. The upper stories might be closed off, but someone lived on the ground level.

They entered a large kitchen area with original cotto tiles on the floors. Something that smelled delicious was cooking in the oven. She was so hungry her mouth started to water.

He removed his helmet, then proceeded to undo the chin strap on hers and pull it off. Callie turned to the side so he wouldn't get it into his head to undo the jacket and take it from her. She was still too aware of his nearness and the way he made her feel when he touched her.

After she'd pulled down the zip and slipped out of it, he took it from her and laid everything on a side table against the wall.

"There's a guest bath at the end of the room. Make yourself at home, then we'll eat."

"Whose farmhouse is this?"

"A friend's. There's a couple further up the hill who take care of it. You and I will sleep here until tomorrow morning when I drive you to the church to be married."

It was no use getting into a verbal fight with him. He wouldn't listen to her. For the moment, the only thing to do was pretend to go along with his wishes until she could work on another plan to escape.

"Come join me," he said when she came out of the bathroom a few minutes later. She took a seat opposite him at the table placed in front of the hearth where a fire was burning. The warmth felt good against the slight chill of the night air.

She ate the veal and pasta with relish, but turned down the wine he would have poured in her glass. Callie didn't drink alcohol. It was just as well since she needed to keep her wits until she could get away from him.

So far she'd seen no bars at the windows. Long after Nicco had gone to bed, she would climb out one of them and run through the woods until she came to a road where she could hitch a ride to Torino.

He drained the rest of his wineglass, then sat back in the wooden chair, crossing his long, powerful legs at the ankles in an almost insolent male gesture.

"You don't need to be nervous about the ceremony in the morning. A priest speaking Italian will perform it in the private chapel of the Tescotti palace with only the prince's family as witness. At the proper moment you'll be alerted to say, 'I do,' in English, and that will be it."

Callie pushed herself away from the table and stood up. "You might drag me in there, but you won't get a word out of me."

His dark eyes flashed her a look of mocking indifference. "That will present no problem. If you are foolish enough to remain mute, the prince will simply answer for you."

Trembling with rage she cried, "I won't wear a wedding dress, either!"

"As you wish, *signorina*. Like you, the prince isn't interested in what you're wearing, or *not*..."

Heat wafted through her from head to toe. "Do you honestly believe God would sanction such a travesty?"

"Since I can't speak for Him, I have no idea." He rose to his feet. "The important thing to remember is that you'll be married in the eyes of the church and the country and of course legally."

While she stood there in frozen frustration, he cleared the table and blew out the candle.

"Morning will be here before we know it. Though you're one woman who doesn't need her beauty sleep,

I'm sure you're tired after your long flight from Los Angeles. The bedroom is to the right of the bathroom. Though not elaborate, it's clean. Follow me.''

Now that she'd eaten and felt revived, she was eager to see it and plan her escape route. But all her hopes were dashed when she entered the sparsely furnished room that didn't look like anyone had slept here in years.

"Which bed do you want? The one by the window or the door?"

"I'm not ready for bed!" she blurted angrily.

"When you are, just remember that the upper floors are closed off. But please don't worry. None of my lovers has ever accused me of snoring or walking in my sleep.

"However if you're frightened that those problems make up part of *your* fatal flaws, I promise I won't tell the prince. Tomorrow night will be soon enough for him to discover your secret delights for himself."

Like a child having a temper tantrum, Callie tossed her purse on the other bed and walked to the window. There were two tall panes of glass which could be opened without difficulty.

"You can try..." she heard him whisper.

When she spun around, she noticed he'd already stretched out on top of the bed near the door, boots and all.

This was never going to work! Without giving him a backward glance, she ran from the room to the door of the farmhouse. Naturally he'd locked it.

As for the windows in the kitchen, they weren't the kind that opened. She was his virtual prisoner.

Feeling as if she'd taken a trip to the outer limits, she sank down on the floor in front of the fireplace. Looping her arms around her raised knees, she stared into the dying flames.

Short of finding a way to incapacitate Nicco, it appeared she might have to wait until she was facing the prince at the altar before she had another opportunity to take everyone by surprise and run away.

But knowing Nicco, he would make certain there were other guards on watch to ensure that nothing went wrong at the ceremony. If she tried to bolt, she probably wouldn't make it out of the chapel doors.

Short of doing something that would cause the prince to cancel the wedding, she could see no way out of this nightmare.

The problem was to think of a strategy that would force his hand.

Her mind went over several possibilities. An hour passed by before she came up with the only idea that just might work. *If* she had the courage to carry it out.

By any standards it was outrageous. So outrageous in fact that under any other circumstances, it would be unthinkable to Callie.

Unfortunately she was desperate.

When the fire had turned to dying embers, she got up from the floor and walked back to the bedroom. Her plan couldn't be put off any longer.

Enough moonlight came through the window to see the outline of her jailer's hard-muscled physique still fully clothed as he lay on the top of the bed.

''Nicco?'' she whispered.

''Si, signorina?'' he drawled.

She swallowed hard, unable to tell if he'd been asleep or not. ''The fire went out in the fireplace.''

''It was inevitable.''

"I realize that. The thing is, I—I'm ready for bed, but I'm used to a much warmer climate. It's cold by the window and the blanket is so thin."

"Then we'll trade beds." In one effortless movement he sprang to his feet. "Get in this one." The next thing she knew, he'd pulled down the sheet and blanket for her.

Callie murmured a quiet thank-you. After removing her shoes and socks, she lay down on the mattress.

Once her head touched the pillow, he covered her before walking across the room to lie down on the other bed. She noticed he'd taken great care not to touch her.

The Nicco of a few hours ago had said and done things to make her believe that given the slightest chance and encouragement, he wouldn't think twice about taking advantage of their situation.

She needed to send out a stronger signal. If she could get him to at least kiss her, then she would tell the prince that the man he'd sent to guard her couldn't be trusted. If she could convince him she'd been compromised, he'd call off the wedding.

Expelling a deliberately troubled sigh he couldn't help but hear, she sat up in bed.

"What are you doing now?" he muttered in a voice that had gone several decibels deeper.

"I'm still cold, so I thought I'd unbraid my hair. It might make me a little warmer."

A sound of male frustration left his lips before he disappeared from the room. The next thing she knew he'd returned with his motorcycle jacket. By now her hair hung about her shoulders.

"Lie down and I'll put this over you."

That wasn't what he was supposed to say. She was

doing this all wrong. Gearing up her courage she said, "Thank you. I'm sure your coat will help. But I'm not used to sleeping alone, and need the warmth of another body."

It was too dark to see his features clearly. "Does the man you slept with as recently as yesterday know you're about to become the sleeping companion of Prince Enzo for the next thirty days and *nights?*"

There was an edge to his tone now. She'd made him angry. That was good. He sounded much more like the dangerous Italian male who'd met her at the airport.

"I was referring to Chloe, the runt of a litter nobody else wanted. The poor little thing was born with a toe missing from both front paws. But since she's not here to cuddle, I was hoping you'd lie down on top of the covers. Just to feel your warmth would probably help me go to sleep."

She had to disabuse him of the fact that she was trying a major seduction scene on him. All she wanted was for him to break down enough to kiss her. But what happened between them needed to seem perfectly natural.

An odd stillness filled the room. He placed the coat over her upper body. "It's not that cold."

"Maybe not, but it *feels* colder to me b-because I'm frightened."

Another silence ensued before he spoke again.

"You don't need to be. The prince won't demand anything of you that you can't give. He signed the contract, too."

She sat up abruptly. "I realize you two are close. Yet behind closed doors no one knows what really goes on between a man and a woman. Even though I believe that *you* believe what you're saying, you truly can't make that promise for another human being. Once I'm forced to marry him, anything could happen," she stammered quietly.

"You're right. It's possible you might find him more attractive than you originally thought and decide you'd like him to make love to you."

He'd purposely twisted her words. Tamping down her frustration she said, "From the picture of him my sister showed me, he looks to be very handsome, but that's not the point. He's a complete stranger to me. I always wanted my first experience to be with the man I loved!" Her declaration bounced off the walls of the room.

"You expect me to believe you've never slept with a man?"

"No. I wouldn't expect anything from you. You couldn't care less if you're holding the wrong woman hostage. What would make me think I could convince you of something that sounds unbelievable, even to me?"

Callie could understand his incredulity. Her lack of experience with men was embarrassing.

She turned on her side away from him and pulled the jacket up to her chin. So much for her femme fatale ploy. He wasn't falling for it.

"Contrary to the old wives' tale, making love is not a fate worse than death. It can be a very pleasurable experience in fact. Surely you're not that naive."

"I understand what goes on well enough, but I refuse to be a guinea pig for the prince's pleasure."

"You should have thought of that before stepping off the plane in Torino."

"I did, but like a fool I was trying to help my sister so I gave him the benefit of the doubt. I should have known he'd send someone else to deal with the situation. I realize you're only doing the job the prince pays you to do, but I was hoping you might show me a little kindness tonight.''

While she waited, she could hear that intelligent mind of his turning things over. It wasn't very flattering.

If Ann had been here, she wouldn't have had to orchestrate anything. Nicco would have been so attracted, he'd have found a room upstairs with a double bed.

Of course if Ann had flown to Italy, she would have told Nicco to take her directly to the prince, so it was all a moot point anyway.

''You're not afraid of me?'' he asked in a silky voice.

''No. The prince obviously trusts you with his life. Besides, any man who owns and rides a Danelli motorcycle only has one mistress on his mind, and it's not a woman.''

A low chuckle escaped his throat before he got on the bed and fit himself right up against her back.

Dear God. What had she done?

One arm went beneath her pillow, the other encircled her and the jacket. It didn't take long for her to feel his warmth through the covers. Whatever soap he'd used in the shower still clung to his skin.

''How do you know so much about motorcycles?'' His breath tickled the skin of her neck, sending darts of awareness through her body.

This wasn't such a good idea after all!

''Growing up we had some wealthy neighbors next door. Their oldest son Jerry owned a variety of bikes which he kept in a special mechanic's garage at the back of their house. I used to hang out in there and talk to him.

"When I got old enough, he taught me how to ride and make minor repairs on them. Pretty soon I was reading all his old motorcycle magazines.

"One day he brought home a beautiful black and yellow Danelli 100 Strada sports bike. I fell in love with it and learned everything I could about them. He made me a promise that if he ever had to sell it, I could buy it from him."

Nicco's arm tightened on hers. "You could only have been about ten years old when that model was manufactured in Milano." Evidently he'd seen her age on either the benefit application or her passport, and had figured the years correctly.

"You're right. Though he got married, Jerry came back to his parents' home a lot and we kept up our friendship. About six months ago he phoned to tell me he was selling his bikes which he kept in mint condition. Did I still want to buy the Danelli Strada? Naturally I jumped at the chance because they're the best bike made."

"I couldn't agree more."

"Do you know it still runs perfectly?"

"That doesn't surprise me."

Why wasn't he going away? "When you're not working for the prince, do you race?"

"I used to, once upon a time."

"For the Danelli company?"

He nodded. "Among others."

It didn't appear she was going to get any more information out of him.

"For a man who's over the hill, you're still pretty good." In truth he was a sensational rider, but she refused to give him that much satisfaction.

"Such high praise. I'm overwhelmed."

"Do you know the owner, Luca Danelli?"

"*Sì,*" he whispered against her cheek. She felt it all the way to the tips of her toes.

Callie scooted away from him and sat up. "Do you know why his company stopped making bikes?"

Nicco eyed her speculatively, as if he was deciding whether to answer her question or not. "His right hand in the business, the man who'd served with him in World War II, passed away unexpectedly. The heart went out of him. He suspended all manufacturing at a time when other companies were starting to spring up."

"I never read about that in my cycling magazines."

"He kept his business private."

"Who was his partner?"

"Ernesto Strada."

Her eyes widened. "That's *his* name on my bike. I thought Strada meant 'street' in Italian, implying it was a street bike."

"Anyone who didn't know the truth would have made the same assumption."

"Mr. Danelli must be quite old by now."

Deep laughter rumbled out of Nicco. "Don't you know there are no old Italian men?"

"If you're suggesting that at ninety he still chases after women, then let me tell you something. Italian men don't have the monopoly when it comes to *that* problem."

His smile was wicked. "You ought to know."

She tried to catch her breath. "Seriously, Nicco— since he has started manufacturing again, do you think when I fly to Milan to catch my plane home, I could take a tour of his factory first?"

"No." He tucked a strand of her glossy hair behind her ear. "Now that he has recommenced operations, all bikes for sale on next year's retail market must remain a secret until they arrive at the various showrooms throughout the world."

"What about the bike you're riding?"

"Mine is this year's racing bike."

She bit lightly on her inner lip. "Doesn't he ever make an exception?"

After a long silence, "If you mean, could I use my connection to Prince Enzo to wangle you a personal tour, *if* I were so inclined?"

Callie nodded.

"Possibly."

"Name your price and I'll pay it," she said before she realized how it sounded.

His hand moved so his fingers could caress either side of her mouth. "Tempted as I am to exact what I want from you, I'm afraid it would break my oath to the prince."

Another tremor shook her body. Before they'd gone to bed, she'd wanted Nicco to kiss her so she could go to the prince with proof that his henchman couldn't be trusted. But in the last few minutes something had changed. She found herself *aching* for a taste of his sensual mouth of her own freewill.

"Does the prince have to know?" Callie couldn't believe she'd just asked him that."

"No, but *I* would."

Expelling a frustrated sigh, she turned on her side so she faced the wall. It appeared that in his own way, Nicco was an honorable man.

His fingers played with her hair. Each movement sent

a little current of electricity cavorting through her system. He brought her body alive.

"I have an idea that would make us both happy, *signorina*."

"What's that?" She struggled to keep her voice steady.

"Don't fight the marriage ceremony tomorrow, and I swear that I'll put in a good word for you with Signor Danelli. In fact if you're an especially obedient bride, I'll let you pick out any bike you want for a wedding present after your honeymoon."

She blinked. "That's very generous of you, but you couldn't afford to give me one."

"Why do you say that?"

"Because the prince has no money to speak of which means your only substantial salary comes from your day job, not from *him*. What you *do* earn certainly wouldn't be enough to buy me a $150,000 bike. This conversation is ridiculous anyway since I don't intend to marry the prince."

"You have no choice, *bellissima*."

"Don't call me that! For your information it's time for you to go to sleep in your own bed now. I'm warm enough with your jacket. Thank you for putting it over me."

"Actually I'm very comfortable here with it covering both of us. Do you mind?"

"Not if you don't care about my snoring."

He tugged gently on a handful of her hair he'd wrapped around his fingers. "If you haven't had a lover, how do you know you make noises in the night?"

"Because my sister *does,* and we're identical."

"No problem," he murmured. "I've become used to Valentino's snoring, so yours won't bother me."

No matter what Callie said, he always had a clever answer for everything.

"I heard him snore outside the door while he was guarding me in the hall. Did you know there's an operation that could fix his problem?"

"I'm afraid the prince likes him just the way he is. The noise is comforting in the dark hours of the night."

"Valentino sleeps with the prince?"

"Every night. Does the thought disturb you?"

"Of course not. I think it's sweet." The prince had just risen a notch in her estimation.

"Most new brides wouldn't want a third party in the bed chamber."

"The prince should have made that point clear to all the potential contestants before the benefit ever took place." Except that it wouldn't have put Ann off. She loved animals too.

"Luckily for him, he picked a woman who sleeps with a runt named Chloe. You and your husband-to-be have something vital in common. That's a good omen for beginning your life together. I can picture the four of you now all snuggled up in the royal bed."

"Then your imagination is a lot better than mine," she muttered as she fought certain images of her and Nicco passionately entwined.

"What kind of a dog did you say yours was?"

"I didn't. She's a pug."

"Ah…a breed well-known for its snoring."

"Yes, and she guards me with a vengeance, too."

"Valentino will be enchanted."

"I don't think so. Chloe doesn't like animals and

other people. Not even my mailman has been able to befriend her, and he's the nicest person I know.''

''Maybe that's because the man who delivers your letters has an interest in you, *signorina*, and your little puplet senses danger.''

So they were back to *that* subject again. ''It's more a case of her having been abused by a male owner.''

His hand stilled on her arm. ''That's too bad, but I wager the prince will win her around.''

''This is a pointless conversation. If you don't mind, I'd like to get some sleep now.''

Her plan to vamp Nicco so he would kiss her simply wasn't working. Even if he had, she would have lost her nerve and pulled away from him. No matter how desperate she was to avoid getting married, kissing a stranger in order to get out of the ceremony wasn't something she could do. She must have been insane to have entertained the idea in the first place.

It was Nicco's fault. He held an appeal for her that was growing stronger with every minute they spent together. At this point she had more than one pressing reason for leaving Italy as soon as possible.

''I wish you sweet dreams, but know you won't need them because in less than twelve hours you'll be a real princess. Your husband-to-be is a very fortunate man. *Buonanotte, signorina.*''

His lips against her temple were more like a benediction, yet they sent another quiver of delight through her body. She held herself rigid to prevent him from divining her reaction.

Despite all his male banter, she knew she was as safe with him as if she were his sister. That should have been reassuring to Callie.

It *was* reassuring. Yet somewhere inside her lived the regret that she hadn't met Nicco under other circumstances.

As she drifted off to sleep, she couldn't help but wonder how things might have turned out had she been a simple tourist, one who happened to catch the eye of a certain exciting Italian male as she got off the plane in Torino.

What if he had pursued her and shown her the city on the back of his bike? In time who knows if they might have fallen in love...

CHAPTER FOUR

"SIGNORINA Lassiter?"

She thought it was Nicco, but his voice sounded far away and he didn't speak to her like the ardent lover he'd been in her dreams.

"Come! This is your wedding day. You don't want to be late. I have coffee and rolls waiting for you."

Wedding day?

Suddenly she was wide awake and sat up straight in the bed.

Instead of being wrapped in his arms as they watched the crashing surf along the Big Sur in California, she'd awakened to the same room of the Italian farmhouse where Nicco had kept her prisoner during the night.

"I'm not hungry!" she shouted to him before jumping off the bed.

"Then let it be on your head if you faint during the ceremony," he said as she slipped on her sneakers.

Good. He was still in the kitchen.

Without wasting another second, she ran over to the windows and opened them. But when she would have climbed out, there was a middle-aged man working in the garden.

"Buongiorno, signorina," he called to her very innocently, but Callie had every reason to believe Nicco had stationed him there to prevent her from escaping.

"Good morning," she murmured before pulling the

glass closed again. There was nothing to do but reach for her purse and make a trip to the bathroom.

While she freshened up and put her hair in a braid, a new plan to get away from Nicco entered her mind. She imagined he would be driving them back to Torino on the motorcycle.

If she waited until they were stopped at a light or held up in traffic, she would jump off the back and run away. It could be dangerous and she might even get hurt. But it would be worth it if she had to be driven to a hospital in an ambulance. Getting injured would prevent that absurd marriage from taking place.

Armed with her latest strategy, she left the bathroom anxious to carry out her scheme. Nicco had already disappeared from the kitchen. Though her stomach growled, she walked past the food he'd prepared for her and kept on going until she'd stepped out the door into the sunlight.

"At last," came his mocking response. "What a lovely autumn morning for a wedding."

We're not at the church yet.

Nicco had already put on his helmet and stood next to his bike. After helping her into his jacket, he slipped the other helmet over her head.

Beyond the bike she saw the truck parked in the drive. She guessed it belonged to the caretaker who'd brought it home at some point during the night. To her chagrin she'd been so sound asleep dreaming about being in Nicco's arms, she hadn't heard any noise.

"This is your special day. I hope you'll enjoy the return ride to Torino. Up you come," he said after he'd gotten on the bike. With a flick of the switch, the powerful engine came to life.

The man in the garden waved them off as they rode past the farmhouse toward the highway in the distance.

Callie groaned in disbelief when two elegant black limousines with flags flying a royal crest appeared out of nowhere to escort them down the mountain. They moved in front and behind Nicco's motorcycle. So much for jumping off the bike and running away.

Though she couldn't see through the smoked glass of the limo windows, she assumed the interiors were filled with the prince's security guards who would make certain no mishap occurred that would prevent her from arriving on time for her wedding.

Naturally Nicco had lied to her about his cell phone needing to be charged. He couldn't have orchestrated these details without being able to communicate.

How on earth was she going to get out of this?

If she faked illness, Nicco would only ignore her machinations and carry out the prince's orders. Panic set in to think she could be kidnapped like this in broad daylight. Their bodies were wedged so closely together, he could check any move she tried to make.

Hundreds of clueless people in other cars watched in rapt fascination as the unique cortege displaying the Tescotti royal emblem passed them by. Even if she screamed for help, no one would hear her. Now that they'd reached the outskirts of Torino, two police cars joined the limos. Their sirens blared, forcing the traffic to give them plenty of space to maneuver.

When she realized they were headed for one of the baroque palaces she'd seen on their way out of the city last evening, a chilling feeling of inevitability crept over her.

If she were a woman inclined to faint, now would be

the time. Unfortunately Callie had a strong constitution. If the prince wanted her for his bride this badly, then he'd have to take her kicking and screaming to the altar.

Too soon they arrived at a gate where a uniformed guard to the palatial estate allowed them entrance. Callie supposed that even if the prince was so impoverished he had to live in an apartment in town, his parents probably occupied a wing of the palace. No doubt it was state-supported by opening up most of the rooms to the public for tours.

She presumed the family retained some privileges, such as use of the royal chapel for christenings and marriages.

Dear God. Marriages... Her marriage. To a total stranger!

The head limousine drove around the heavily wooded estate to a private road leading to a side entrance of the ornate palace. Nicco stayed right behind it, then finally pulled to a stop and levered himself from the bike.

By the time he'd helped her to the ground, a dozen uniformed guards surrounded them. He handed one of them his helmet.

"I'll relieve you of these," Nicco explained before removing the jacket along with Callie's purse and helmet. Another guard stood by ready to take them.

She swallowed with difficulty. "Nicco—please don't make me do this."

He stared at her through veiled eyes. "It's only for thirty days, remember? If after that time you want a divorce, you can walk away, no questions asked."

Tears threatened. She fought to keep them from spilling down her cheeks. "But this whole thing is a terrible mistake. If you would make one phone call to my sister, you would find out the truth.''

His lips tautened. "It's too late for the truth. You *will* marry the prince this morning. Once we pass through these doors, we'll take a walk down the hall. It leads to the chapel. I'll accompany you to the altar and tell you when to say I do.''

By this time Callie's moist eyes were spitting green sparks. She couldn't believe this was happening to her.

He could read her mind. "If you make any struggle or cry out, I will toss you over my shoulder and keep you there until the priest pronounces his benediction. Do you understand?''

She threw her head back. "This is madness!''

A cruel grin broke out on his unforgettable face. "I couldn't agree more, but it's what the prince wants.''

"He must be the most spoiled male on the planet!''

"As his wife, I'm sure you'll be the first to find out. Do you need to use the ladies' room before we go any further?''

"No!''

"Very well. Put your hand on top of mine.'' He lifted his arm.

Heat scorched her cheeks. "I won't do it.''

No sooner had the defiant words flown from her lips than he did exactly what he said he'd do and threw her over his shoulder.

"Put me down, Nicco!''

Ignoring her protest, he walked through the doors held open for them. As her head bobbed and her braid swung back and forth like a pendulum, she caught glimpses of snowy white marble floors and gilt-edged mirrors lining

the long promenade to the chapel where she could hear
an organ playing.

"You can't carry me in front of the priest like this!"

"He's the least of your worries. Naturally he and the
prince's family will assume you're typical of your na-
tionality...flaunting your lack of respect for tradition on
the prince's wedding day.

"Americans are noted for their uncivilized behavior.
Your noisy presence on my shoulder will simply under-
line all that is unflattering and undesirable about your
kind."

"How dare you say that to me! If you were in my
shoes, I can guarantee you'd do anything you could to
escape!"

"*Signorina*—now it is you who has the better imagination if you can see me in your predicament."

"Stop!" She grabbed hold of his rock-hard thigh with
both hands, trying to hold him back. He just kept going,
not seeming the least out of breath. "Please, Nicco. I'm
begging you. Put me down."

"You already had your chance."

"I'm asking for a second one. You win—all right?"

He paused before the golden bars of the chapel gate.
"How do I know this isn't another of your creative
tricks?"

"You don't...but I have no wish to offend God who
will hold you and the prince responsible for this crime."

"I'm willing to accept His punishment," his voice
grated. "So is the prince who is waiting impatiently for
you to make an appearance."

On that note he lowered her to the stone floor. He
could probably feel her trembling outrage. *And fear.*

She took a last look around. There were security guards everywhere.

No place for you to run, Callie Lassiter. This is the zero hour. Time to get it over with. You still have an opportunity between the ceremony and your wedding night to run away from the prince.

Without looking into Nicco's eyes, she faced the golden bars. Instead of him offering her his arm, he clasped her hand. No doubt he'd changed his mind in order to make certain he had a good grip on her in case she'd lied to him and decided to make a run for it.

"Once we pass through this gate, we'll proceed to the center aisle, then turn toward the altar and walk the short distance. Let's go," he said as one of the guards opened it for them.

With Nicco half dragging her, she was forced to take her first steps. It reminded her of a science fiction film where this couple from the future grabs hands and jumps off an exploding planet into a beam of light, not knowing what will happen to them. Callie felt exactly like that frightened woman.

Until they came to the center aisle, she kept her eyes on the scarlet runner covering the marble. When Nicco turned them toward the altar, she chanced a look ahead of her and was dazzled by the sight of the royal family bedecked in ceremonial dress, gowns and jewels.

Brown-haired Prince Enzo stood in front of the shrine of the small chapel. In his wedding finery, he was even more handsome than the picture Ann had shown her.

On his left stood a very pretty, young-looking brunette in a long white gown wearing a coronet. Nicco hadn't mentioned that the prince had a sister. Next to her were two beautifully dressed women in their late fifties or early sixties, also brunette. One of them also wore a coronet. Obviously it was the prince's mother. Possibly the other woman was an aunt.

Callie's gaze swerved to the two middle-aged men standing to the right of the shrine. The aristocratic one with black hair was dressed in clothes similar to the prince. He had to be his father though they didn't appear to resemble each other that much. Callie presumed the man next to him was an uncle or close relative.

As Nicco tugged her along, an elderly priest in his vestments took his place in front of the august group. It seemed to be the signal for everyone else to turn around and watch Callie and Nicco's approach.

Though she'd been literally kidnapped here against her will, the gravity of the occasion didn't escape her, nor the fact that she looked ridiculous and out of place in such a sacred setting.

When compared to the Tescotti family, she couldn't help but reflect on her miserable attire. Jeans, sneakers and a cotton top would never be appropriate for a wedding. To wear them in a church, in front of royalty no less, verged on sinful. However she couldn't do anything about it now except hold up her head until this ghastly experience was over.

The wedding processional music accompanied them the rest of the way, increasing her sense of humiliation even though none of this was her fault or doing.

In touching distance now, Prince Enzo reached for her free hand. After eyeing her soberly, his mouth broke into a kind smile before he bestowed a princely kiss on top of it.

Ann had been right about him. He did seem nice, and he had the most beautiful brown eyes and attractive dimples she'd ever seen. It was his right hand man Nicco who was the cunning mastermind behind this storybook scene.

While the prince made room for her to stand next to him, Nicco stayed at her other side, never letting go of her hand. The whole situation was so ludicrous, Callie could have sworn she'd landed in the twilight zone. Anyone watching would think she was being married to Nicco.

The priest began to speak in Italian. Except for the fact that she knew she was being married to a prince who looked like he'd come right out of the fairy tale *Snow White*, she had absolutely no idea what the priest was saying.

Surely a man as appealing as Prince Enzo could have won the heart of any girl, Italian or otherwise. Not for the first time did Callie wonder why he'd picked an American woman for his bride. Someone who wanted to be a Hollywood film star more than anything else.

Being this close to Prince Enzo, she had the strongest conviction he hadn't chosen Ann for the money she would bring to the marriage from her films. Otherwise he wouldn't have put that thirty-day clause in the contract which would allow both of them to bow out if they didn't want to be married anymore.

None of it made sense. Ann brought no land, no crown, nothing to cement a political marriage as in the days of old.

Something wasn't right here. Callie just didn't know what, and Nicco wasn't helping anything by making small circles against her palm with the pad of his thumb.

Perhaps he didn't realize what he was doing, but the motion was more like a caress, and it was driving her crazy. She tried to ease her hand out of his, but he only increased the pressure until she couldn't move her fingers at all.

She was so preoccupied by the way his touch made her senses come alive, she scarcely understood the thrust of his words as his lips brushed her ear and he whispered, "It's time to say, 'I do.' If you refuse, I'll say it for you."

The priest's benign eyes rested on her.

Much as she wanted to scream that she had been brought here under duress, she realized the priest wasn't to blame for any of it. Only God knew the secrets of this day. He was the judge of this perfidy. In time both Nicco and the prince would have to answer to Him.

"*You* go ahead and tell the priest I do," she whispered back to Nicco in a baiting tone.

A satisfied smile broke out on her captor's face. In a surprise move he pulled the betrothal ring out of his pocket and slipped it on the ring finger of her left hand. Then he said something else in Italian to the priest who nodded before turning to address the Prince.

For a fleeting moment she had the impression that maybe she was marrying Nicco instead of Enzo, but surely not.

Nicco couldn't be a prince.

Callie tried to listen to Prince Enzo's response, praying he would back out at the last moment. To her chagrin, Nicco squeezed her hand, distracting her. It seemed he was relieved to have done his part for his employer.

He'd done it all right!

Not only had he managed to get her to the altar—with those few simple words and the ring, he'd helped the prince to lock her into the kind of forced marriage you read about in history books.

It wasn't until she heard the organ begin to play that she realized the ceremony was over. The priest made the sign of the cross before walking down the aisle. The Tescotti family followed.

While Callie was waiting for the prince to turn to her, she found herself being commandeered by Nicco who pulled her along. Without anyone else being aware of it, he squeezed her hand, forcing her to keep up with him.

Wondering what was going on, she looked over her shoulder and discovered Prince Enzo following them out of the chapel with his sister on his arm.

Evidently Nicco feared Callie might make a scene and run away from her new husband, so he was still her captor and the normal protocol for a royal wedding couple marching down the aisle together had been abandoned.

She imagined he wouldn't let go of her until he'd taken her back to the prince's apartment. First however, she had to pass through the small receiving line in the mirrored galerie.

The priest stepped forward. "My congratulations, Princess," he said in heavily accented English. "May God's blessings be upon you."

Princess Tescotti.

Callie moaned. Could anything be more absurd?

"Thank you, Father," she murmured back.

Nicco whispered something private to the priest in Italian. To Callie's surprise the older man answered back in English, "It was a great honor, my son."

"Niccolino—"

The woman who looked so much like the Prince broke

out of the line to embrace him. Obviously Nicco was held in great esteem by Enzo's parents. Tears of happiness rolled down her cheeks. She spoke in rapid Italian and a lengthy conversation between the two of them ensued.

Finally he turned her toward Callie. In English he said, "May I present Callie Ann Lassiter from America who is now a part of the Tescotti family."

The older woman kissed Callie on both cheeks, unaware of her turmoil. "I thought this day would never come. We've been praying for such a long time, haven't we, Carlo," she said to her husband who was standing next to them.

At close range Callie couldn't see a resemblance to his son, not with his black hair.

The Prince's father kissed her on the forehead. "My son has picked a beautiful bride who appears perfectly suited for him."

Perfectly suited? Was the prince an aspiring actor? Maybe that was why he'd chosen Ann, because he thought he could get into films with her help. Why hadn't she thought of that sooner?

"After your honeymoon, you must come to the palace so we can all get acquainted."

Again Nicco answered for her, but he spoke in Italian. Whatever he said caused the older man to nod.

By now Callie was fuming. If Nicco thought he'd outmaneuvered her, he had another think coming. Little did he know there wasn't going to be a honeymoon. As soon as she could be alone with the prince, she'd figure out a scheme to get away.

For the moment, she was still Nicco's prisoner.

He introduced her to the next couple, explaining they

were close friends of the family. The four of them shook hands before he ushered her out the side door of the palace where his motorcycle stood parked between the two limousines.

Evidently not a single word was going to pass between her and the prince until Nicco had her well secured back at the apartment.

That was fine with her! She would climb out one of the windows and escape even if it meant tying some sheets together.

While she was picturing it in her mind, two of the guards handed them their equipment. She put her purse around her neck and donned her helmet. Nicco followed suit, then slipped on his jacket.

Once he'd climbed on his bike, he turned to help her get on. At his signal, the lead limo guided them along a private road to another guarded gate at the rear of the estate. Soon their motorcade joined the main street and made its way along the boulevard at a fast pace.

They traveled a good fifteen minutes before Nicco suddenly made a left turn, leaving the limousines and heavy noon traffic behind. He drove the bike into a private marina leading to the river.

They went down an embankment toward a shady spot where a small barge was moored. A narrow plank of wood made it possible for Nicco to drive right on to the boat from the shore.

Only an expert biker on a supreme machine like the Danelli could have performed such a faultless maneuver without having an accident. He moved her and the bike to the side of the barge where he propped it and helped her down.

While she took off her helmet, he pulled the plank

onto the floor of the barge. Shocked because they hadn't gone back to the prince's apartment, she watched in a daze as Nicco undid the ropes and cast off. Only then did she realize she'd missed an opportunity to jump ashore and get away from him.

The river looked deeper and swifter than she'd first supposed. If she dove into the water now, she might not make it to safety.

"I wouldn't try it if I were you," he muttered before disappearing inside.

Within seconds she heard the motor start up. What plan had he and the prince hatched now? Determined to have it out with Nicco, she entered the cabin.

The boat was no royal yacht. She had to remember what Nicco had told her. The prince couldn't afford anything more expensive, yet it contained the essentials like a bathroom, kitchen, living room.

And bedroom.

All the comforts of home. Callie would have loved it if she were on a real honeymoon with the husband she adored.

Nicco sat in the forward engine room with the door open. He had removed his jacket and helmet. His disheveled black hair along with the shadow of a beard against his olive skin should have made him less attractive. But somehow they underlined his stunning masculinity until she couldn't look anywhere else.

He sat sideways in the captain's chair. His piercing black eyes narrowed on her features.

"Welcome aboard the *Serpentina,* Princess. I happen to know you must be starving. You'll be happy to hear that around the next bend in the river, Prince Enzo will be joining us. Then you can eat."

She lounged against the doorjamb. "You're good at what you do, Nicco. No wonder he employs you to carry out his dirty work. While you're at it, why don't you return this to him."

For the second time in twenty-four hours she relieved herself of the betrothal ring and tossed it at him. In a deft move he caught it and put it in his pocket.

"Is there anything else I can do for your highness?"

His taunting drawl was the last straw. Feeling a trifle nauseous, she wheeled around and went back out on deck. After watching the wake for a moment, she decided it was making her sicker.

She closed her eyes and clung to the rail. The weakness she was experiencing didn't have as much to do with hunger as it did an impossible situation.

Nicco had managed to cut her off from civilization. Here she was hidden away on some river thousands of miles from home, at the mercy of two unscrupulous men who were playing a diabolical game at her expense.

She hadn't been far off when she'd suspected the prince of having a streak of madness in his genes. Today she'd been forced to marry him. But that didn't mean she would sleep with him!

There had to be some life preservers on board. As soon as she found one, she'd jump over the side and swim for help.

Spying a foot locker, she ran toward it and lifted the lid. Sure enough, there were a dozen or so preservers along with some rope and a paddle. Without hesitation she reached for one and put it on.

After she put the top in place, she used it for a step to get up on the railing.

"Going somewhere?" Nicco's familiar male voice

spoke before two arms of steel pulled her back against his hard-muscled physique.

"Let me go!"

"Before you do anything as rash as throw your body in the river, I suggest you hear what Prince Enzo has to say. He's waiting for you in the cabin."

Callie blinked.

Sure enough there was no engine noise. They'd pulled up to the landing while she'd been unaware of it.

"I'll relieve you of this." In a swift move, he freed her from the preserver. "Do you need assistance to walk?"

She tried pushing him out of the way, but it was like attacking a wall of granite.

"If you don't want your behavior exploited in the tabloids, try to behave with some decorum. Not only his bodyguards, but members of the press are watching from the shore taking pictures."

"Good!" she fired back. "Maybe they'll figure out I've been kidnapped!"

"Actually they heard about your reaction at the airport yesterday. Watching you almost fling yourself into the shadowy depths will have added truth to a growing rumor."

"What rumor are you talking about?" she blurted in fury.

"That the prince has managed to marry an incredibly shy virgin. I assume they're having a good laugh right now."

"Then let's hope they choke on it!"

So saying she stormed back into the cabin and came face-to-face with Prince Enzo.

He'd changed into tailored trousers and a sport shirt.

Without all the trappings, he looked like a guy her age who was totally approachable. His face broke into a gentle smile.

"*Signora*—before you say anything, I want to thank you for being in that Hollywood benefit and following through on your commitment to me. Because of you, I'm now married to the woman I love.

"While Maria and I are on our honeymoon, be thinking about something we can give you in return. Something you want but would probably never buy for yourself."

Maybe it was because she felt so faint that Callie thought he'd said he was going on a honeymoon with someone named Maria.

"I don't understand. Didn't you and I get married today?"

She could hear a limousine horn honking outside.

"Yes, but not to each other. I have to go now. My brother will explain everything."

"Who's your brother?"

He frowned. "Nicco didn't tell you?"

"Not yet," Nicco spoke up behind them. "First we're going to eat, then talk." He said something else in Italian that made the prince grin before he disappeared out the door.

"Shall we?" Nicco held a chair for her.

Confused and bewildered, she sank down on it and stared at the sandwiches and salad Nicco must have put out for them while she was looking for a life preserver.

Nicco sat opposite her and poured them both a glass of wine. For once in her life she decided she needed a strong drink and took several swallows.

"Better now?" he inquired.

"Not really." Still holding her wineglass she said, "Would you please tell me what's going on?"

"I'll be happy to as soon as we've finished our lunch."

"I won't be able to eat a bite until you explain what Prince Enzo meant. If he married the brunette woman I thought was his sister, then the only man I could have married in that chapel was *you*."

"Si, signora."

The wineglass slipped from her fingers and fell to the floor of the barge. Fortunately it only broke in two pieces. Nicco picked them up and put them on the table.

"That's impossible! The priest called me Princess."

"Father Luigi has a twisted sense of humor."

"Perhaps he does, but he wouldn't have said it if it weren't true. Dear God…you forced Enzo to trade places with you because *you're* the prince!"

His arresting face darkened with lines. "An accident of birth. When I turned twenty-five, it was my duty as the firstborn Tescotti to accept the throne and marry a girl my parents had chosen for me. But I wasn't in love with Princess Benedetta and knew the life of a royal wasn't for me.

"Therefore I renounced the throne along with my properties and money. Unfortunately my father chose to take that action personally. I couldn't convince him that my decision had nothing to do with my love of our family.

"We quarreled and I left the palace with only the clothes I was wearing. With his marriage today, my brother Enzo has inherited everything I rejected."

Brother?

Suddenly an image of his dark-haired father swam

before her eyes. Certain things Nicco had said to her yesterday came rushing back to her mind.

This close to the ceremony I have sworn a sacred oath to protect you with my life. In fact I am the only person in the world who has Prince Enzo's complete trust.

"I should have guessed at the relationship between you two long before now." She raised troubled green eyes to his. "Now I'm more confused than ever. If Enzo was already in love, why in heaven's name did he go all the way to Hollywood pretending to be looking for a woman to marry?"

Nicco's expression grew bleak. "Because *I* needed a wife."

"I'm sorry, but this isn't making any sense to me. My sister signed a document with his name on it."

He shook his head. "If you'll take time to read the marriage document carefully, you'll see my legal name as the prince you promised to marry, not Enzo. He went to Hollywood to confuse you. It was a risk that paid off. You were right about my Machiavellian tendencies."

Callie's thoughts reeled as she remembered a certain conversation with her sister.

This morning, before I flew up here, I asked my attorney to look over the contract I signed. He says there's no way I can get out of it. That's why you're the only person on the planet who can help me.

Ann's attorney hadn't even caught the mistake!

Nicco darted her an enigmatic glance. "Enzo should have married Maria on his twenty-fifth birthday and inherited the throne I rejected. But Father was so embittered over what I did, he refused to give Enzo his blessing. He was hoping I'd change my mind.

"Last month I found out Enzo and Maria were expecting a baby. At that point I realized something had to be done so Father would allow them to wed with the blessings of the church. I spent the night thinking about a plan, then went to see my father the next day.

"After disabusing him of the notion that I wanted my title back, I explained that at long last I'd met *the* woman for me. As a concession to my parents, I consented to be married in the family chapel provided it could be a double wedding so Enzo and I could take the leap together."

No matter how many scenarios Callie could have conceived of, what she'd just heard would never have come to mind.

"Ten years of my living away from home seemed to have mellowed Father enough that he finally agreed. Naturally I was elated for Enzo, but I found myself in a dilemma of a different kind."

"You mean because you're allergic to *marriage* as well as thrones."

"*Sì.*"

CHAPTER FIVE

NICCO sat back in the chair eyeing her shrewdly. "As I told you yesterday, you're more intelligent than I had originally assumed."

The knowledge that he preferred his bachelor status shouldn't have hurt so much. It shouldn't have hurt at all!

"You're very clever yourself, Nicco. No wonder you chose some dim-witted American from Hollywood who loved the limelight and wouldn't expect to stay married when she found out you were a has-been prince."

His lips twitched, provoking her to retaliate.

"You're in luck because you signed the contract with my sister Ann, not me."

"You still insist you have a twin." It was a rhetorical question.

"Yes. Fortunately for you, she wants no part of anything that doesn't have to do with acting, so you're off the hook.

"Now that I've stood in as a surrogate fiancée and done my part for God, country, Ann and the Tescotti family, I'm off the hook, too, and can get back to my busy life in Prunedale."

Having made her declaration, she reached for a chicken sandwich and devoured it. "Um, this is really good. You should try one." After eating another half, she filled her plate with fruit salad and dug in.

He stared at her for a moment. "Tell me about this Prunedale. I've never heard of it."

She swallowed the last of her salad, then said, "Few people have who don't live in the state. It's a farming community in Northern California. Lots of orchards and animals."

"You must like them in order to have made an instant friend of Valentino."

"He's gorgeous."

"So...if you truly aren't an actress, dare I ask if you're a farmer?" He was toying with her now. While he waited for her response, he ate a sandwich.

She bestowed a brilliant smile on him. "Certainly you can dare. However the answer is no."

Something flickered in the recesses of those black eyes. "Aren't you going to satisfy my curiosity?"

"Maybe I will if you'll satisfy mine first."

"What is it you want to know?"

"How soon can we leave for the airport? I'd like to catch a commuter flight to Milan before the day is out."

"I'd like nothing more than to accommodate you, but your thirty days aren't up yet. During this period we must convince my parents we're madly in love and intend to make our marriage work."

Her face felt hot. "We're not legally married."

His black eyes impaled her. "I'm afraid we are. When you told me to tell Father Luigi 'I do,' you sealed your fate whether you go by Ann or Callie Ann. If you have any doubts, ask the priest."

She didn't have to. There'd been a point during the ceremony when she'd had the strangest presentiment that she was marrying Nicco. Last night she'd dreamed about him being her husband. Shades of prophesy?

"For all intents and purposes, we've already made a good start. By appearing at the church in the same clothes you slept in on the plane, you've shown that you're as much of a rebel as your new husband.

"Needless to say, no self-respecting Italian woman with the kind of royal pedigree my parents chose for their firstborn to marry, would have shown up looking like you did today. It added an authentic touch that worked well for us."

My son has picked a beautiful bride who appears perfectly suited for him.

Finally she understood his father's left-handed compliment.

Nicco seemed to be reading her mind because he added, "That's why you must stay the specified time in the contract. If you leave Italy before a month has gone by, my father will know this was a trick."

"It was a trick on a par with Machiavelli himself!" she bit out hotly. "I want no more part of it."

His features hardened. "You already are. I'm afraid you joined me in this dangerous game when that contract was signed.

"For myself I have nothing to lose. However the consequences of a rash decision on your part will come down squarely on the head of my little brother who's an innocent pawn."

Alarmed by his words, even if it had been Ann who'd gotten Callie into this trouble, her heart started to pound faster. "What do you mean?"

"Exactly this... If you desert me before my father believes we've given our marriage a chance to work, he'll exact his revenge by taking Enzo's title away from him."

"Why?" she cried out aghast. "I thought you said his heart had softened a little over the years."

"To a point. But if he found out it was all a ruse on my part, he wouldn't hesitate to hurt me by hurting my brother.

"Unlike me, Enzo always wanted to ascend the throne and be the kind of king to make the family proud. He has many ideas for reform. Ideas that need to be put forward.

"You could have no comprehension of how much he dreams of being a hero in my father's eyes, but he can never achieve that if his whole world is cut out from under him.

"For a new husband, that would be a particularly bitter pill to swallow. For a young royal returning from a honeymoon to face that kind of pain while his vulnerable bride is looking to him for help because their baby is on the way, it would constitute a living death."

He drank the rest of his wine before pushing himself away from the table. "If your conscience can handle breaking the contract I assumed was signed in good faith, then by all means *leave* before I cast off. Your passport is back in your purse.

"Just be aware that a swarm of reporters is still on the shore taking pictures of us embarking on our honeymoon. They'll pick up on any breath of royal scandal. But if that's what you want before my brother's plane has even left the tarmac..."

How arrogantly male of him to try to make her feel guilty. "*I* wasn't the one who signed that contract!"

He sent her a withering glance. "I once knew a pair of identical twins. They felt the same pain at the same time. When one was cut, the other bled. When one needed help, the other sensed danger and came to the rescue.''

''I *did* come, and look what happened!''

He shrugged his shoulders in typical Italian fashion. ''Things could be worse. You could have exchanged vows with a man who *wanted* to be married.''

Oddly wounded by his statement she said, ''But how convincing will it be to your parents if it's all over in a month's time anyway?''

''When the thirty days are up, the press will receive a riveting piece of gossip. There will be a picture of the heartbroken elder son of the Tescotti family whose American wife has decided they need a separation because of irreconcilable differences having to do with their nationalities.

''The sympathy of the monarchy will be on my side. Father won't be able to prevail against it, and Enzo will be allowed to fulfill his destiny. With Maria at his side, at least there'll be one person in the Tescotti family who's finally living his dream…''

''Hi. Sorry I'm not in. Leave a short message and I'll get back to you when I can.''

''Ann? It's Callie. I know you can hear me, and I know you haven't left for work yet. In two minutes I'm going to ring again, so please pick up. This is impor—''

''Callie?''

''Thank goodness you answered. I don't have a lot of time.''

It wasn't exactly true, but she was using Nicco's cell phone which was miraculously working again. The last thing she wanted was to get into a long, personal conversation with her sister while he was watching and listening.

"I assume you're on your way home. Don't worry. We can talk later. I'll pick you up at L.A. airport tonight just as planned."

"No—that's why I'm calling."

"What's wrong? You sound funny. Is the prince giving you a hard time?"

"Look, Ann—it's a long story. Just so you know, I—I'll have to stay in Torino for the next thirty days."

She heard a whoop coming from the other end of the phone. "Does this mean what I think it means?"

"No—" Callie blurted. "At least, not exactly. Well, yes. In a way. You see—"

"Oh my gosh!" Ann cried. "You fell for that dreamy prince and got married! I can't believe it!"

Nicco was sitting next to her on the couch. He unexpectedly leaned closer so that she could feel his warmth. "It's my turn," he whispered before taking the phone from her.

She relinquished it with a trembling hand.

"*Buongiorno*, Annabella."

After his greeting, there was silence on his end. At least now he would realize Callie really did have a sister and had been telling the truth all along.

"This is Nicco Tescotti. Callie told me you are the twin who met my brother in Hollywood at the benefit. I understand you're a rising film star."

No one's English sounded more seductive than Nicco's with that Italian accent. As for his comment to Ann, he couldn't have said anything guaranteed to please her more.

Wondering what was coming next, Callie lowered her

head. To her shock he slid his arm around her shoulders as if it were the most natural thing in the world.

"If my wife sounds confused, it's because she married me instead of Enzo. When he sent me to the airport to pick her up, it was love at first sight for both of us. I have to thank you for sending her in your place. It had to be destiny."

Don't, Nicco.

"After spending the night together, we decided to make everything legal. It was a double wedding. Enzo married his childhood sweetheart."

Callie's groan reverberated throughout the cabin. Nicco held her tighter.

"Now that we're related, I'm anxious to meet you, too. Hopefully we'll get together soon. Just so you know, for the next while Callie and I will be on our honeymoon. *Incommunicado.*

"But we couldn't leave without telling you the happy news first. I'll give you back to your sister now. She's dying to talk to you. *Ciao,* Annabella."

He handed Callie the phone.

"Ann?"

"Well, well, well. Still waters really do run deep. You're royalty now. Wait till I tell everyone on the set my sister is Princess Tescotti."

"I'm not a princess, Ann. Nicco renounced the throne years ago."

"He sounds exciting, if you know what I mean. How old is he?"

"Older than his brother."

She felt Nicco's lips against her cheek. "I'm thirty-five."

"As long as he's not in Dr. Wood's age bracket," Ann teased.

Callie's breath caught in her throat. If her sister ever met Nicco, she'd think he was the sexiest male alive.

"The way he handles his Danelli, Nicco's not in his dotage quite yet."

"He owns a motorcycle?"

"I've driven it," Callie bragged. For that remark, she received a squeeze on the arm, reminding her of her crime.

"Now I understand how this happened so fast. Do me a favor and fax me a picture of him."

"I—I'll try. Listen, Ann—I have to hang up now."

"Wait— Just tell me one thing. Knowing it was your first time, how was last night?"

My big seduction scene turned into a disaster.

"We'll have to talk about that later. Bye." She hurriedly clicked off. Nicco's gaze swept over her rather thoroughly before he took the phone from her and stood up.

"Before we cast off again, I'm sure you'd like a shower."

"I would. Thank you."

"I'll take one after you. Everything you'll need is in the bathroom. There's a cupboard with a clean pair of sweats you can put on. Later we'll do a wash."

"You even have a washing machine?"

"It's vital for long trips."

Thankful for that bit of news, she rose to her feet and reached for her purse that held her toiletries. "I had no idea a barge could be this comfortable."

"I bought it several years ago and have been outfitting it in my spare time. River travel in Europe allows you to see sights you'd never discover otherwise. As it is, the press won't be able to invade us on our three-day honeymoon.''

Her heart gave an extra beat. Three days alone with him?

''The best they can hope for are some shots of the barge using a telephoto lens.''

By the time she'd reached the bathroom her brows had knit into a frown. She turned on her heel. ''Does the paparazzi hang around you all the time?''

''You don't want to know.''

''But you refused the crown years ago!''

''I'm afraid once a prince…''

Callie groaned. ''How awful.''

''If they decide to get daring and chase us in another boat, we can always elude them by taking the bike on a side trip.''

The motorcycle meant a lot more to him than his love of the sport. It represented his freedom in a way that most of the world would never understand. ''No wonder you brought it on board.''

''After a hard day's work, there's nothing I crave more than a ride.''

He was talking to the one person who understood. ''What do you do for a living?''

''Nothing I don't like.''

With that comment he'd told her absolutely nothing!

''Do you realize there are only a few people on earth who can't tell their pleasure from their work?''

''When I was twenty-five, I decided to find out what that would be like.''

She took a deep breath. ''Have you found happiness?''

Shadows crept into his eyes. "That's an interesting question. I'm not certain such a state truly exists."

A few minutes later she was still pondering his lonely comment as she stood under the shower to wash her hair.

The more she learned about Nicco, the more she could see that in choosing a different path than that of his family, he'd suffered in the process. Still, she couldn't help but wonder if he wasn't struggling with another kind of problem, too. One that had given rise to his aversion to marriage.

A woman perhaps?

Whoever had brought Nicco Tescotti to his knees had to have been someone remarkable. Unforgettable. No matter what had transpired between them, their failed relationship had left a deep scar.

Oh, Ann—when you begged me to come to Italy in your place, I knew I was flying into danger. I just hadn't counted on a tortured prince in Italian leather stealing my heart the moment I laid eyes on him.

Suddenly Callie regarded his comment about a press release to advertise the heartbreak of the Tescotti family's elder son in a whole new light.

When she left Italy in a month, there was going to be heartbreak all right. *Hers.*

For the next three days they traveled the waterways of the Dora Riparia, Sangone and Po rivers. Though Nicco had warned Callie the press would be monitoring their progress, the matchless scenery of the hillsides and Alps caused her to forget that the rest of the world existed.

From morning till night they ate and lazed about in the fall sunshine. While she feasted her eyes on various landmarks—trying hard not to stare at his compelling profile—he drove the barge and filled her head with fascinating information.

More than a tour guide, he'd led the privileged, well-traveled life of an educated royal who could relate little known facts that brought the history of this part of Europe alive for her.

"Every time we go around another bend in the river, there's a glorious new sight. It's so heavenly, Nicco, I could travel this way forever."

"You know what Le Corbusier said—"

"The French architect?"

"*Sì, esposa mia.* It's his considered opinion that our city has the most beautiful natural position of any in Europe."

"I agree!" she cried, aware that she was effervescing too much, but Callie didn't know where to go with all her burgeoning emotions. Every minute spent with Nicco was pulling her under his spell a little more. The fact that he treated her like his best friend's sister was killing her.

Though he'd wanted to stay far away from the prying eyes of the paparazzi, he knew what he was doing by getting her alone on the barge. Inside the cabin he was free to be himself. No worry about having to pretend to be in love with his new bride.

Every night after dark, they'd tie up at a landing and he'd go to sleep on the couch. She slept safely in his double bed, hoping he'd find some excuse to join her, if only to talk, but he never did.

"What's the name of that mountain in the distance?"

"The one behind Valentino Castle is Mount Rosa, the second highest in Europe after Mont Blanc."

"Valentino— He's *your* dog!" Of course he was.

"Sì." Nicco's lips broke into a half smile.

"You named him after this castle?"

He eyed her through veiled eyes. "You thought erroneously that it was inspired by the famous Italian lover of the American silent films?"

She looked away quickly, wincing from the trace of cynicism she'd just heard. "I didn't know."

"Valentino Castle is one of the domains of the House of Savoy. Maria Cristina, the daughter of Henry IV and wife of King Victor Amadeus I of Savoy, had it rebuilt according to her French taste. Below the Parco del Valentino is the famous Cerea Rowing Club.

"The area we're passing through serves as a course for the Silver Skiff race when the various historic rowing clubs compete."

"Did you ever race?"

After a long silence, "Once upon a time."

That was the second time he'd used that expression. She shouldn't have asked him a question that reminded him of his past, but she couldn't seem to help herself. With a powerful physique like his, he'd probably mastered several grueling sports.

Being the firstborn son of a royal family, he'd probably been expected to do many things without having any choice in the matter. Callie couldn't fathom such a life.

They passed beneath the Isabella bridge and came upon the central section of a submarine which he explained was a relic from World War I. Beyond it was a restaurant converted from a World War I dredger.

Another bridge came into view. "One day if there's time before you return to the States, you'll have to go through the National Automobile Museum you can see there on the left bank. It houses vintage cars and motorbikes you'd find of particular interest.''

The way he said it let her know he wouldn't necessarily take her to see it himself. Reading between the lines, it sounded as if he didn't want her to forget that the time of parting would be here before she knew it.

So don't get too comfortable with me. Is that what you're saying, Nicco?

Stung by his comment, she left him at the wheel and walked outside the cabin to stand at the railing. The trees along the riverbank were starting to cast shadows from a setting sun.

In a few minutes they moved toward a private marina in the distance where he drew alongside some moorings. A man who worked there tied the ropes while Nicco bridged the barge to the shore with the wooden plank. As he lowered it into place, it made a thudding sound that echoed in Callie's aching heart.

Her honeymoon was over.

If they'd been lovers, no bride could have asked for a more idyllic three days.

"Callie?" It was the first time he'd called her by her correct name. She loved the way he pronounced it with an emphasis on the last syllable. "Come put on your helmet. I want to get out of here before every reporter in Torino descends on us."

She hurried inside for her purse, then scrambled to do his bidding. Within minutes she'd climbed on behind him. Displaying his usual expertise, he drove off the barge and up the embankment in one smooth sprint. On the way out to the street they passed several television vans turning into the marina.

Nicco hadn't exaggerated about the media. How

ghastly to be dogged like this every time he appeared in public.

She felt him change gears. As if he'd shifted to warp speed, they shot forward. On the short ride to his apartment, it was surprising to her that their tires ever touched the ground.

When his building came into view, she thought they were home free, but she was wrong. Once he'd turned into the driveway, they were forced to deal with a barrage of flashes from photographers who'd probably been hiding near the bushes for some time, waiting for a glimpse of Nicco and his new bride.

Like lightning he drove around back to his parking stall. They both jumped off the bike and he hustled her inside the building past one pesky reporter holding a microphone.

To her surprise and disappointment, Valentino wasn't there to greet them when Nicco unlocked the front door of his apartment for her to enter.

She pulled off her helmet and put it on the side table in the front foyer. "Where's your dog?"

"At the other end of the hall. I'll ring the Loti's. Their son Giovanni watches him for me. He'll bring him along."

"Can't we go get him instead?"

Nicco removed his helmet and jacket. His eyes swept over her in swift appraisal. "If you want to come face-to-face with that reporter, be my guest."

Callie shook her head. "You mean they actually have the gall to come inside the building?"

"They do anything they want if they're hungry enough."

"So that's why you had the police escort me to the

Get FREE BOOKS and a FREE GIFT when you play the...

LAS VEGAS GAME

Just scratch off the gold box with a coin. Then check below to see the gifts you get!

YES! I have scratched off the gold Box. Please send me my **2 FREE BOOKS** and **gift for which I qualify.** I understand that I am under no obligation to purchase any books as explained on the back of this card.

386 HDL DUYJ   186 HDL DUYY

FIRST NAME

LAST NAME

ADDRESS

APT.#

CITY

STATE/PROV.

ZIP/POSTAL CODE

(H-RA-03/03)

7	7	7	Worth TWO FREE BOOKS plus a BONUS Mystery Gift!
🍒	🍒	🍒	Worth TWO FREE BOOKS!
🔔	🔔	♣	TRY AGAIN!

Visit us online at www.eHarlequin.com

Offer limited to one per household and not valid to current Harlequin Romance® subscribers. All orders subject to approval.

The Harlequin Reader Service® — Here's how it works:

If offer card is missing write to: Harlequin Reader Service, 3010 Walden Ave., P.O. Box 1867, Buffalo NY 14240-1867

BUSINESS REPLY MAIL
FIRST-CLASS MAIL   PERMIT NO. 717-003   BUFFALO, NY

POSTAGE WILL BE PAID BY ADDRESSEE

HARLEQUIN READER SERVICE
3010 WALDEN AVE
PO BOX 1867
BUFFALO NY 14240-9952

NO POSTAGE
NECESSARY
IF MAILED
IN THE
UNITED STATES

apartment that first day. Anything to avoid more scrutiny from the press.''

He nodded. ''Drastic measures were called for to keep our wedding plans a secret from the public. However now that I'm married, the press has learned about it and is clamoring for close-ups of you.''

''Then let's give them what they want so they'll go away.''

He darted her an enigmatic glance. ''You don't mind?''

''I haven't lived with it before, but since you want to convince your parents we're happily married, then what will it hurt? If we don't run from the press, maybe they'll show us some mercy. We'll just bluff our way through any questions asked. It might even be fun.''

He looked like he'd never heard the word before.

There was a prolonged silence as Nicco rubbed the back of his neck where several tendrils of black hair clung to the nape. Little whorls she'd wanted to unravel with her fingers while he drove the boat.

''I'll leave it up to you to do the talking,'' he finally muttered. ''Let's go.''

Callie had never looked a worse mess. Right now she was minus any makeup, and her braid was coming loose. As for the clothes she'd worn on the plane, Nicco's parents would wonder if she had another outfit to her name. But in the end, none of it mattered as long as Enzo's dreams were realized.

One thing she did know. Nicco loved his brother and had proved it by going through with a marriage he wanted no part of. Knowing all the facts, Callie really would have been a selfish monster if she hadn't agreed to stay the month for Enzo's sake.

Now whom are you trying to convince, Callie Lassiter? You little hypocrite! If you weren't in love with Nicco, you'd have jumped off the barge and disappeared three days ago.

Angry with herself, she opened the door first and stepped out in the hall.

CHAPTER SIX

"HEY, Princess—look this way!"

She turned her head toward two reporters who took a dozen pictures in succession.

"Come on, guys. I tell you what," she said to them, still dazed by the flashes. "If you promise not to call me princess, I'll be happy to cooperate with you. My name is plain old Mrs. Tescotti who is married to plain old *Mr.* Tescotti.

"I'm a new bride, and just like any other bride, I would like to have a few days privacy in my own home with my brand-new husband.

"If you would pass the word around, then any reporter who wants to come here two weeks from this evening at six o'clock is welcome. Provided there are no more incidents of you jumping out of doorways, I'll invite you in and give you a half hour to take pictures and ask questions. How does that sound?"

"Will your husband be here, too?" the other reporter asked.

She felt Nicco move behind her. He slid his arms around her waist. "Of course."

More flashes went off.

"Thanks! *Molto grazie!*" they said in both languages before leaving the building.

When quiet reigned he whispered, "You managed to perform a minor miracle just now."

His comment thrilled her. So did his arms that tightened briefly before letting her go.

"Let's get my dog, shall we?"

She could have cried to find herself free again.

Callie walked down the hall with him, afraid he could hear her heart pounding too hard. He'd never know how much she'd wanted him to go on holding her.

Nicco rapped on the end door. Behind it she could hear voices. The minute it opened, Valentino came charging out in the hall to greet his master with great yelps of joy. Three days' separation was a lifetime to an animal who was loved. Callie had been feeling the pangs of being away from Chloe since she'd left her with Dr. Wood.

A teenage boy and his mother followed. The two of them spoke in rapid Italian to Nicco before he introduced them to Callie. Though the mother was very warm and cordial to Callie, she seemed upset about something. The boy looked anxious too.

"What's wrong?" Callie whispered.

"A few days ago they brought their cat home from the hospital. Now it's sick again and they have no car to transport it back there because her husband is out of town. I told them to crate it and I'd take it on my bike."

Without conscious thought Callie said, "Can I see your cat, Giovanni?"

"*Sì*. Come this way, *signora*."

Forgetting everything else, she followed the teen through the small apartment to the kitchen where their large, grayish brown Norwegian forest cat lay on the floor, lethargic as could be.

Callie knelt down beside it. "What's his name?"

"Figaro."

"Oh, poor Figaro. You're a lovely cat," she murmured as she examined it. "What was wrong with him before?"

"The doctor said he got dehydrated," the boy answered. "He was fine when we brought him home. Now he's sick again."

"Bring me its water, will you?"

"*Sì, signora.*"

The teenager quickly did as she asked and set the cat's bowl of drinking water next to her. Figaro didn't make a move toward it. Callie put her fingers in the liquid, then cajoled the cat to lick the moisture. At first the animal hesitated, but eventually it began to respond.

Over and over again she dipped her fingers in the water, then put them to the cat's mouth. Little by little it became more animated until it began drinking from the bowl itself.

She gazed up at Giovanni. "Your cat is thirsty. Have you kept her bowl of water out for her at all times?"

"*Sì.*"

"Do you know why she hasn't been drinking from it?"

The boy turned to his mother who spoke little English. He asked her the question. After she answered he said, "Mama thought Figaro must be sick again."

"But didn't you tell me the doctor said the cat was dehydrated before?"

"*Sì.*"

"So how long has she been staying away from her drinking bowl?"

He spoke to his mother who at this point was wringing her hands. "She says she doesn't know. Most of the time the cat climbs up on the sink in the bathroom to drink."

"You mean you fill the sink for her?"

"No. The tap has dripped for months and months, but a few days ago my father finally fixed it."

"Ah…that explains it."

By now Nicco was down on his haunches next to her. Valentino squeezed in between them. "Explains what?" he asked. His dark, expressive eyes searched hers for a heartstopping moment.

She smiled at him, then the boy and his mother. "Figaro is a creature of habit. He got so used to taking drinks from the bathroom sink, that when he couldn't find any more water dripping, he simply stopped drinking."

Giovanni laughed before telling his mother. Soon everyone was laughing, including Nicco.

"You must retrain your cat to drink from his water dish. Stay with him tonight. Help him to lick the moisture from your fingers until he realizes you want him to drink from the bowl all the time.

"If you see him head for the bathroom, turn him around. Though it may take a few days for him to get the point, he'll be all right by tomorrow."

Giovanni grinned. "Mama says you are a genius."

Callie chuckled. After scratching behind the cat's ears, she got to her feet. "I wish I were. In this case I'm just glad I could be of help. It was very nice to meet all three of you."

The *signora* thanked her and pumped her hand repeatedly. Giovanni did the same. Finally Nicco suggested they leave. After the door closed they walked down the hall of the apartment together in companionable silence. Valentino got in the middle and paced himself to stay even with them.

The second they entered Nicco's apartment he shut the door. In the next breath he'd put his hands against the wall on either side of her so she couldn't go anywhere. The boxer looked on expectantly.

His gaze played over her face. "How did you know what to do? I don't want to hear that it's because you love animals. I already deduced that the moment you met Valentino."

She eyed him steadily. "Would you believe me if I told you?"

After the laughter they'd shared moments earlier, his grave expression surprised her. "I suppose I deserved that."

"There's no great mystery, Nicco. I'm a vet."

He studied her as if she were some kind of a puzzle he hadn't begun to figure out yet. "In Prunedale," he said at last.

"Yes."

"Evidently I should have been addressing you as Dr. Lassiter all this time."

She shook her head. "Like you, I hate titles. Dr. Wood calls me Callie."

"Dr. Wood?"

"He heads the North Monterey County Animal Hospital. I work for him and live there."

Something flickered in the recesses of his eyes. "You *live* there?"

"In a back room."

"Does he live there too?" Nicco's voice drawled.

"Next door."

"How convenient." His sarcastic tone was too much.

"It is!" she fired back. "I'm going to have to live cheaply for the next ten years to pay off my medical school loans. He's my landlord as well as my boss, and has made it possible for me to earn my living and save a little money at the same time.''

"Do you do his cooking, too?" he asked in a deceptively mild voice.

"Sometimes."

More often than not he fixed food for her. It was a hobby of his since his wife had passed away. He was a much better cook than Callie ever hoped to be, but she wasn't about to admit that to anyone.

A thoughtful expression crept into Nicco's darkly handsome face. "No doubt he expected you back several days ago."

With him standing so close to her, she could hardly breathe. "Not really. Ann cleared it with him before she ever talked to me about her problem. My sister made up a story that I'd won a month's vacation in Europe or some such thing. He was kind enough to give me the time off.

"In actuality *I'm* the one who expected to turn right around and fly back. The Selanders's mare is ready to foal and I wanted to be there for the delivery.''

"Instead the black prince of the Tescotti family has you locked up in his own private dungeon." He stared her up and down. "If I hadn't forced you to marry me, you'd be back on the job you love right now."

She averted her eyes. "Yes."

"Surely Dr. Wood will be able to handle being apart from you twenty-seven more days."

Tired of his taunts she cried, "He can handle anything!"

One black brow lifted. "Well, with that kind of testimonial, I'll stop feeling guilty for depriving him of his remarkable assistant any longer than necessary.''

Callie could have sworn Nicco didn't have a penitent bone in that incredible male physique of his.

"In fact after witnessing the way you diagnosed Figaro's problem within seconds of examining him, I would say Dr. Wood's loss appears to be our gain in more ways than one. Isn't that true, Valentino?''

He finally let her go and leaned over to rub his boxer's ears. The dog barked as if he understood every word. Maybe he did. Callie had worked with animals long enough to know there was a telepathic connection between them and humans. The recent shows on television of the woman pet psychic had led Callie to believe anything was possible.

Suddenly Nicco lifted his head and stared hard at her. "You wouldn't have mentioned Valentino's snoring problem if you weren't concerned about it. What's wrong with him?''

She bit her lip. Valentino meant the world to Nicco.

"Let me ask you a question first. Did you raise him from birth?''

His jaw hardened. "No. Eight years ago I found him behind the rear of the apartment looking half dead from hunger and neglect. He was just a puppy, probably not even weaned from his mother yet. I brought him inside and took care of him. By the time he'd recovered, I couldn't part with him.''

A man after her own heart.

"Your dog's breed has a snoring problem, Nicco. If you catch it early on, some of the flesh can be removed at the back of the throat to relieve the blockage. If left, labored breathing can result later on in life.

"After eight years of Valentino not being able to breathe at full capacity, I'm uncertain whether an operation at this late date could fix the problem."

Lines marred his features. "The vets at the clinic where I've taken Valentino have never mentioned it."

"When they were in vet school, it probably wasn't emphasized. In all fairness, I didn't realize how serious snoring could be in short-nosed breeds until after I started working for Dr. Wood. He continues to teach me things that were glossed over in class."

He stroked his dog's back. "If I could arrange for it, would you do the procedure on Valentino right away?"

Callie's eyes widened in astonishment. "You mean here? In Torino?"

"Where else? If we were to fly to California so you could perform the surgery there, Valentino would have to go into quarantine for weeks first. I don't want to make him wait that long to relieve his misery."

Callie closed the expanse between them and knelt by the dog. She smoothed her palm over his beautiful head.

"He's not as miserable as you suppose. His difficulties have come on slowly and grown with him. As I said, an operation might not improve his condition. On the other hand, it could lengthen his days."

"By how much?"

"Anywhere from six months to two years depending on his general health. Boxers usually live ten to fourteen years. But you must remember something. Though the risk is minimal, some animals don't survive a general anesthetic."

His black eyes trapped her gaze. "What if he were your dog?" It was as if his soul were reaching out to hers.

She swallowed hard. "I wouldn't hesitate to do whatever I could to improve the quality of his life."

"That's what I thought. Tomorrow we'll see about it."

Her hand stilled on the dog's head. "Nicco—I doubt any vet hospital would allow some foreigner to come in and use their facilities. It's just not done."

"You're right, but I know a place where there won't be a problem."

"Where is that?"

"The Tescotti estates are very large with many animals. Father retains a vet who takes care of them. There's an operating room at the stable with everything you'll need."

Her head reared back. "I thought you—"

"So did I," his deep voice cut in on her. "But I've just discovered I'm not above using my family after all. Not when it comes to Valentino's welfare or my brother's."

"What do you mean?"

"When I phone my father to ask his permission for my veterinarian wife to use the hospital's facilities to cure my dog, he and Mother will be convinced our marriage has substance. That's a plus for Enzo I hadn't counted on before you and I left on our honeymoon."

Callie looked away and stood up. If his parents were like most people she knew, they'd have a hard time understanding how a marriage that seemed to get off to such a good start could suddenly fall apart a month later.

It was one thing to be photographed as Nicco's wife where his parents would see her in the newspapers. But it was quite another to act the part of his loving spouse on the royal estate where news of them being on the grounds would travel directly to the palace. Callie didn't like that idea at all.

"I—I don't think you shoul—"

"The matter is settled," he interrupted her in a steel-edged tone. Traces of the prince still lingered no matter how hard he'd tried to distance himself from his unique heritage.

She took a fortifying breath. "Won't your father's vet be hurt when he finds out you've brought in someone else?"

Nicco shot her a defiant glance. "You're my wife. He'll have to handle it."

So saying, he walked to the foyer for his helmet and jacket. She and the dog followed.

"While I'm gone, go ahead and eat what you want from the fridge, it will have been stocked up while we were away. If you feel like a shower, there's hot water for two minutes only, so be warned."

She tried to hide her smile as she imagined how different life had been for him since he'd left the palace for good.

"When you're ready for bed, use my room. You're welcome to any of my clothes. Tomorrow we have a lot to accomplish including a move, so get a good sleep."

A move?

Before she could ask him what he meant by that exactly, he'd disappeared from the apartment, leaving her alone with a dog who made moaning sounds because his beloved master had gone.

Something told her Nicco had decided to pay a visit to his parents. He probably wouldn't be back for a while.

Callie felt just as abandoned as the dog. After four

days and nights, she'd been spoiled by his constant presence.

"Come on, Valentino. You can sleep with me. I know I'm a horrible substitute, but what else can we do? I need comfort, too."

Valentino followed her around until she'd climbed beneath the covers of Nicco's bed in one of his T-shirts. As soon as she'd settled, the dog climbed on the bed and nestled next to her, placing his head on her leg.

She put out her hand to rub his ears. In the darkness, he snored just like Chloe. It was almost like having her dog back, except that Chloe was smaller and slept on top of the covers between Callie's legs. Still, she derived great comfort from Valentino and knew nothing else until morning.

Before Callie had gone to sleep, she'd had every intention of getting up early the next day to fix breakfast. Though their temporary marriage was in name only, it was time she pulled her own weight. So far Nicco had done everything for her, including the cooking.

But when Callie put on her clothes and went into the kitchen, she discovered Nicco was already up and dressed in another T-shirt and a pair of jeans that molded his powerful thighs.

His dark hair still looked damp from the shower. He smelled wonderful. So did their breakfast of ham and eggs.

There was fresh bread on the small dinette table. He'd probably bought it at a corner bakery earlier that morning.

Valentino looked up when he saw her, then dropped his head and went on eating his dry dog chow as if it were the last meal he would ever have. She and Nicco chuckled at the same time.

In the next breath his dark eyes wandered over her in slow appraisal. "Never separate a dog from his food," he murmured as he sipped hot coffee.

"Never," she whispered in a shaky voice, scrambling for the other chair before she fell down. When he looked at her like that...

Maybe he didn't know what he was doing, but she could hardly function. Afraid he would realize what kind of an effect he had on her, she helped herself to the food he'd prepared and began eating.

"As soon as you're through, I thought we'd do some shopping at a department store so you won't have to live in one outfit for the rest of the month."

She nodded, but didn't talk. Her mind was too busy remembering a certain conversation they'd waged at the airport. Nicco was probably remembering it, too.

You won't be taking me anyplace because I have no need of a new wardrobe.

Then you truly are a dream come true, signorina. I will let the prince know you intend to keep him happy in the marriage bed for the entire thirty days and nights.

"I—I was going to suggest that we stop someplace," she said before digging into her eggs.

"After we're through, we'll come back here for Valentino and drive him to the stable for the operation."

Her eyes darted to his. "You've arranged everything that fast?"

"It's all set. Father spoke to Dr. Donatti. The surgery will be free for our use after lunch."

"He must have been surprised to hear from you."

"Shocked would be more like it. He and Mother both

got on the phone. I told them we cut our honeymoon short to deal with Valentino's problem. When they found out you were a vet, they couldn't have been more eager to help us.''

She detected a nuance in his voice. "What's troubling you, Nicco? Did they sound too happy?"

"Something like that."

"You mean you're afraid they're going to hurt Enzo by putting pressure on you again to take back your title?"

Nicco shook his dark head. "No. For once in their lives they didn't have a word to say about that."

Callie was trying to put two and two together.

"Then you must be referring to our marriage. They're too happy about *it*. Is that what you're saying?"

His expression darkened like a thundercloud, telling her everything she needed to know.

"Unfortunately you're feeling major guilt because marriage isn't for you, and you can't wait for it to end. I'm so sorry, Nicco. I guess when you and Enzo were working on your plan, you didn't consider this aspect of it.

"I realize now that the last thing you want to do is disappoint your parents again. But I've been thinking about it, and there is hope."

"How so?" His voice grated.

"Well, for one thing, they're going to become grandparents in the near future. A new baby will take away some of their sadness."

His stony silence not only alarmed her, it prompted her to keep talking to fill the void.

"Some day they'll become reconciled to the fact that not every man is cut out for married life. I've lived with you long enough to realize you're the epitome of the perfect bachelor. You don't need a woman.''

His eyes had narrowed until she could barely see their color.

"Nicco, it's no sin. I know a few men who wouldn't trade their single status for anything. Their freedom is much too important.

"Perhaps what you ought to do after I go back to my life in California is hook up with some of your buddies and take your girlfriends to the palace for dinner or some such thing.

"Let your parents see that you enjoy women, but after being married to a foreigner of all things, you've decided you never want to be tied down again. In time they'll realize you really are happiest when you're on your own and—''

He muttered something in undecipherable Italian that brought her up short before he pushed himself away from the table. "When you can pause long enough to finish your breakfast, we'll go."

In a few swift strides he left the kitchen. Valentino made a whimpering noise and padded after him.

"Hey—don't be so upset. I was only trying to help you feel better."

Callie dashed into the living room after him, but he wasn't there. She made a detour to his bedroom where she found him tossing some clothes into a duffel bag.

"If I said something to anger you, I apologize. In truth, I've been skirting around the real reason why I think you're down on marriage."

He paused for a moment. "And what would that be?"

"It's none of my business, of course, but I have this feeling you've been hurt by a woman. If you don't want to talk about it, that's fine with me. But if you do, I'm here.

"A lot of my patients' owners tell me I'm a good listener when there's a problem they need to talk over. Technically speaking, Valentino's my patient, so if you have the urge..."

"I have several," he confessed silkily, "but now is not the time to indulge them. Stay, Valentino," he admonished his dog. "We'll be back soon."

Nicco lifted his head unexpectedly. Their eyes met. "After you, Signora Tescotti."

Ooh. He really was upset to call her by her married name.

When they reached the foyer she looked for her helmet, but it wasn't on the side table.

"Don't worry." Nicco read her mind with ease. "I put our gear out in the back of the truck."

Callie nodded and walked out to the carport ahead of him. There in his parking space stood the old blue truck she'd seen once before. Apparently Nicco had ridden to Monferrato last night to bring it here. She'd wondered how they were going to transport the dog to the stable.

He threw his duffel bag in the back, then opened the passenger door for her. Once they were both strapped in, he took off.

Though it was a far cry from his bike, he drove it with the same speed and expertise. How he managed to park it in a tiny space along a major street without damaging fenders was anyone's guess. She simply closed her eyes and waited for the screech.

It never came. Instead it was her heart that skidded all over the place when he opened her door to help her out of the truck. Thinking she would get down by herself, she made a move forward, but it only caused their bodies to collide. His strong hands encircled her hips.

The contact whipped up a forest fire inside her.

Too limp from excitement, she literally slid down his hard-muscled frame until she felt her feet touch the sidewalk. A little moan of unassuaged desire escaped her lips. Fearing he'd heard it, she wheeled away from him so he couldn't look into her eyes and read the secrets there.

To her chagrin, her cheeks went hot as flame. Without waiting for Nicco, she entered the department store ahead of him and marched straight toward the casual wear she could see on her left.

He'd told her it was a moderately priced store where she'd be able to buy everything she needed. Callie didn't require a lot. Just a couple of pairs of jeans, tops, several changes of underwear and nightwear.

Nicco caught up to her and followed her around. He translated prices for her into English and generally drove her crazy by just being near her. While various saleswomen and female shoppers stared at him and did literally everything they could to get him to look at them, she tried to concentrate on making her purchases.

It was an impossible task because she couldn't help casting him covert glances to see if he was responding to all the attention he was receiving since they'd entered the store.

More than once he caught her staring at him. It was humiliating. She turned away, pretending she hadn't noticed him. At one point he suggested she buy a pair of tan leather sandals which he thought would make a nice change from her sneakers.

Other than that, their shopping spree turned out to be

a rather silent affair. Disastrous even, because ever since he'd helped her down from the cab of the truck, she'd felt tension building between them. It sent her pulse racing off the charts.

Unable to take any more, she decided she'd bought enough things and headed out of the store with her purchases. If he touched her again to help her get in the truck, she'd melt like butter and he'd be in no doubt of his power over her. She'd do anything to avoid that situation.

Oddly enough, she ended up sitting there for ten minutes while she waited for him to come. When he showed up, he had some more packages. They were probably items he needed.

After stashing them on the seat next to her, he started up the engine and they returned to the apartment.

His head swerved in her direction. "Stay here. I'll bring Valentino."

She watched him put all their packages in the back of the truck before he disappeared inside the building. Within a couple of minutes, the two of them emerged.

When Nicco opened the door of the cab, Valentino climbed in and sat between them, alert to everything going on.

"Your dog doesn't know he's not a person."

Her comment produced the first smile she'd seen all day. When Nicco's sensual mouth curved up like that, she felt like the sun had just come up over the horizon.

"Are we going to the same estate where we were married?"

"No. The stables are located on a piece of property bordering the Po where Enzo and Maria will live now that he's prince. My brother's an accomplished rider. So is his wife.''

''Do you ride, too?''

''Before I left the palace, I enjoyed it on occasion.''

''Anyone who owns a bike like yours probably enjoyed a lot of other things once upon a time.''

Again she glimpsed his white smile. ''You understand what few women do.''

''More women would *if* they learned to ride on a Danelli to begin with. The bike is perfect for my work. When I go out to the farms to see a sick animal, I strap on my medical satchel and zoom around like a torpedo. There's no other sensation like it. I can go anywhere, even into the fields.''

''Rocket science at its most creative.''

Callie laughed. ''I'm sure the people who know me think I make a queer sight. Ann calls me the mad vet. With my helmet, little children sometimes ask me if I'm from outer space.''

Nicco's chuckle warmed her heart as he drove the three of them to an idyllic, heavily wooded area off limits to the public. Half a mile past the guarded gate of another Tescotti palatial estate she glimpsed a riding path through the trees.

Once all this had been Nicco's playground and would have been his for the taking. But for him it came at too high a price. Like some animals, Nicco was meant to be free.

She'd spent enough time with him to realize he was his own man in every way. That's what went to make him the most attractive male she'd ever met. Her heart ached with love for him, for everything he'd been through and suffered in order to arrive at the place where he was today.

Without conscious thought she put her arm around his dog and hugged him close to her.

"Valentino—I know you don't have any idea what's about to happen to you. But I promise that when you've recovered, you're going to feel a lot better."

"So will I," Nicco murmured, sounding immersed in thought.

The road continued to wind around until she saw what looked like an eighteenth-century hunting lodge. She said as much to Nicco.

"That's because it is. My grandfather had a portion of the interior converted into a small hospital with the stable at the rear. However he insisted that the exterior retain the integrity of the original structures on the property."

"It's beautiful," she whispered. "Like going back in time."

Except for one man on horseback, she saw no other sign of activity. Not waiting for Nicco, she jumped down from the cab and looked up at the giant trees which had probably been here for centuries. They dwarfed everything.

"Nicco!" a male voice called out. Callie saw an older man with salt-and-pepper hair wave to them from the massive front door which stood open. He broke into a spate of Italian.

Her companion answered back before sending her a private glance. "That's Dr. Donatti. He and his wife Bianca live in the upstairs apartment. Father asked him to assist you."

She nodded, realizing this was a delicate situation that

needed special handling. Valentino must have picked up the smell of the hospital on the vet because he hung back against Callie's legs and had to be ordered to accompany Nicco before he would walk inside the lodge.

"I know just how he feels," she whispered to Nicco. "It's the same sinking feeling I get when the dentist tells me to come in because he's ready for me."

Nicco squeezed the back of her neck in response before ushering her inside beneath a vaulted foyer. Her body was still quivering from the sensation as she looked around and saw that one side of the lodge opened up into a large sitting room. It was filled with period furniture, tapestries on the walls and an enormous fireplace.

The other side turned out to be a dining hall with a huge table, hunt board and elaborate chandelier. A couple of her married friends would kill to find authentic hand-carved furniture like this in the States.

"Dr. Donatti, this is my wife, Callie."

"What a pleasure this is for me, *signora*. Congratulations on your marriage."

"Thank you."

The elderly vet shook her hand and smiled, but she was cognizant of his speculative gaze. Callie felt distinctly uncomfortable invading his turf.

Being with Nicco made it so much worse because though he'd given up his title years ago, he was probably still considered the rightful prince by everyone on the estate. Dr. Donatti had no choice but to be gracious to what he undoubtedly considered the black sheep of the Tescotti family.

"We don't want to keep you from your work any longer than we have to. If you would be kind enough to show Callie the operating room."

"Of course. Come this way. My wife is anxious to meet you. She'll be back from town shortly."

Callie followed the vet through the doorway at the end of the foyer. Beyond it she entered the kind of territory familiar to her. From an anteroom he led her directly to the surgery. It wasn't that different from Dr. Wood's inner sanctum.

While she discussed what she intended to do, Nicco entered the operating room with a very frightened, unhappy dog. She left the doctor's side to greet Valentino.

"Come on, boy," she urged as his master had to pick him up and order him to lie still on the table. "I'm not going to hurt you. Dr. Donatti? If you'll please tranquilize him, we'll get started."

Once the dog had been given a shot, she took an X ray, then went over it with the other vet who nodded when she pointed out the problem.

"It's just as I thought, Nicco. Valentino has an overly long soft palate that interferes with his larynx. I'll take some tucks and that should do it." Of course it was more complicated than that, but all that mattered was to get the procedure over and done with as quickly as possible.

The three of them donned gowns and masks. "If you'll administer the anesthetic, we can begin, Dr. Donatti."

Callie felt Nicco's eyes on her as she scrubbed at the sink. Her heart skipped a beat out of fear. She knew how crazy he was about his dog.

Please, God. Let Valentino be all right. Please.

"Everything's ready," Dr. Donatti murmured.

She lifted her hands to put on sterile gloves, then turned to her precious patient and began the operation.

Like Dr. Wood, Dr. Donatti made an exceptional assistant, anticipating every need. For Nicco's benefit Callie explained everything she was doing.

The procedure didn't take long. After she'd finished up, she glanced at Nicco who was standing at the end of the table. She couldn't be sure but she thought he looked a trifle pale. Unsteady even.

Who would have believed Nicco Tescotti of all men had an Achilles' heel?

Moving swiftly, she caught hold of his arm and walked him over to a stool pushed against the wall. Once she'd forced him to sit, she untied his mask.

"Put your head down and breathe deeply."

CHAPTER SEVEN

WHEN Callie returned to her *other* patient, Dr. Donatti had untied his mask. She undid the top strings of hers. They flashed each other conspiratorial smiles that bonded them at a deeper level.

Lifting her stethoscope, she listened to Valentino's breathing. So far so good.

Dr. Donatti reached out to pat her arm. "Don't worry. Niccolino's dog is going to be fine. He was in expert hands."

The fact that the vet had spoken her husband's name like an endearment told her how much he cared for the elder Tescotti son. Dr. Donatti knew how frightened she was for Nicco's sake. If anything happened to Valentino...

"It's been an honor to work with you, Doctor. Thank you for *your* help," she whispered, fighting tears.

"The honor was all mine." He sounded as if he meant it.

"I'm going to stay here with Valentino until he wakes up. Do you think you could take Nicco to the kitchen for something to revive him?"

He winked. "I was just going to suggest it. When he was a youngster, he always did have a tender spot for animals. He dragged everything in here from a rabbit with a torn ear, to a pheasant with a broken wing.

"With his face glistening wet, Nicco would beg me to fix them, then run outside because he couldn't stand to watch. When Enzo came along, he was much the same way.''

''What are you two whispering about?'' came a weak sounding male voice in the background.

''I was simply telling your wife what an excellent job she did. Now I'm thirsty and wouldn't mind a cup of coffee. Come with me, Nicco. By the time we return, your dog will be awake.''

''Go on,'' she urged Nicco. ''I won't leave his side.''

''I'll be right back,'' he vowed before following the doctor out of the surgery. Poor Nicco. She should have realized what a traumatic experience this would be for him. It would have been better if he'd stayed in the common rooms of the lodge until the operation was over.

True to Dr. Donatti's prediction, after a little while Valentino began to stir. Overjoyed, Callie took his vital signs again. All was well.

Though the back of his throat would be sore for about two weeks, he was going to be fine. *Better than fine.*

Finally the dog's eyes opened.

''Good afternoon, Valentino. I'm so happy to see you're awake. Don't be upset with your IV. I'll take it out later. How's my boy?'' She smoothed her hand over his head. ''You've been such a perfect patient. I love you.'' She kissed the top of his head.

''Keep that up and he won't be my dog anymore.''

Nicco's voice sounded much stronger than before. The dog heard his master and lifted his head, then made a moaning sound.

Callie grinned. ''There's no chance of that happening. See how he looks at you?''

Nicco joined her and ran an affectionate hand down

Valentino's back. "Thanks to you, he just might live a year or two longer."

In the next breath Nicco pulled her against him and planted a warm, firm kiss on her astonished mouth.

It felt so right and natural, she found herself kissing him back.

Before she knew how it happened, her lips opened to the persuasive pressure of his. Relief over the happy results of the operation must have been the reason she went pliant in his arms and tried to get closer to him.

In the process, the tenor of their breathing changed. The jubilance they were feeling seemed to translate to passion as their kisses grew more feverish. One melted into another until she didn't know the difference anymore. They couldn't seem to get enough of each other.

"Nicco, darling?" a woman's voice called out from the doorway. "Oh— Forgive me—"

Somehow Nicco managed to recover without problem. He put Callie at arm's length with a calm she could only envy.

"It's all right, Mother." His gaze, which seemed to have been glowing like hot fires seconds earlier, left Callie's and darted to the door. "Come in. I was just thanking my wife for performing such a successful operation on Valentino."

Callie blushed to the roots of her ash-blond hair. To think she'd actually offered herself to him like that, and then to be well and truly caught by the one person who shouldn't have been witness.

Though Callie understood why Nicco had gotten carried away, his mother would assume their honeymoon was still in full flower. She took a step backward so he would have to relinquish his hold on her.

"If you want to continue, we'll leave and come back later, son."

Now Callie understood from whom Nicco had inherited that mocking tone in his voice. His father had observed their prolonged embrace, too. Oh how she wished he hadn't.

Needing to do something with her hands, she started to remove her hospital gown. To her horror, she realized she was wearing the exact same outfit she'd worn to the wedding.

Even though she'd bought some new outfits, she hadn't bothered to change because she preferred operating in her old clothes. His parents didn't know that of course, and would think she was the most bizarre person they'd ever met.

Feeling out of her depth, she reached for the stethoscope and took Valentino's vital signs once more. While Nicco and his mother talked together, his father walked around the table and came to stand next to her.

"How's the dog faring?"

"He's fine so far."

"Was there any doubt in your mind?"

"You never know anything positively." Her voice shook.

"Nicco has total trust in you. Coming from that headstrong son of mine, it's the highest compliment you could be paid. We're very happy he married such a wonderful and accomplished woman. Welcome to the family, Callie. May I call you that?"

"O-of course."

His father's sincerity felt so genuine, she winced in pain. When it came time for her to leave Italy, she was going to feel the wrench.

Today shouldn't have happened! Everything was getting much too complicated.

She knew that deep down Nicco had been worried his parents would take their marriage too much to heart. Now she was worried too. Petrified.

"My son tells me you lost your father and mother a long time ago."

Callie started to shake and couldn't stop. "Yes."

"Maybe one day soon you'll be able to look on me as a true father and call me Papo. Perhaps when you and Nicco make a baby?"

By now Callie was dying inside. There wasn't going to be a baby! A month from now she and Nicco would no longer be a married couple. The whole thing had been a mistake from start to finish.

"Callie?" His mother appeared at her other side, preventing her from having to answer his father's impossible questions. "Please will you use your influence with our son and come to dinner at the palace this evening? He says you have other plans, but surely you could drop by for an hour?"

All she could do was take her cue from Nicco. "We'd love to come, b-but I don't dare leave Valentino for a while. Could we postpone it for another time?"

Maybe as long as she and Nicco had promised those journalists they could come by the apartment for a story, it might be wise to get everything over with on the same day. Then never again!

"That would be lovely. We'll call later and make the arrangements." She patted Callie's arm before stroking the dog's head. "You're invited, too, Valentino, so mind your new mommy and get better."

New mommy—

''Remember what I said,'' Nicco's father whispered. He gave her a warm hug. Then he bent to Valentino's level.

''You're in the best of hands.'' He kissed the dog behind his ears.

The whole attractive Tescotti family were animal lovers. Callie would have liked them anyway of course...

By nine-thirty that night, Valentino was awake and wanted to leave the surgery. Callie removed the IV and pronounced him recovered enough to go home.

Throughout the rest of the day she'd spent a lot of the time discussing other cases with Dr. Donatti while they kept a professional eye on the dog. As for Nicco, he paced the floor so often, they told him to go for a horseback ride. Thankfully he took their advice and rode for several hours.

While he was gone, Callie had time to ponder his kiss of gratitude. Like the lovesick fool she was, she'd turned it into something else. Her response probably had everything to do with his restlessness.

How foolish she'd been to let it go to her head like that. Nicco had to be regretting his own impetuosity. If she left Italy tomorrow, there would be no more incidents of that kind. Unfortunately the news of her departure would create fresh trauma in the Tescotti household, especially for Enzo and his wife.

But maybe while Nicco was out riding, he'd decided he preferred risking that kind of turmoil to being forced to live another twenty-four hours with a besotted wife he didn't love. He hadn't planned on her caring for him when he'd drawn up that awful marriage contract.

If he were counting the hours until he was free from

bondage, Callie would oblige him by leaving as soon as possible. Though she'd lost her heart, she still had her pride. It would see her through until she could be alone to grieve.

Yet the idea of a permanent separation was unthinkable. She couldn't fathom putting thousands of miles between them now.

Try to imagine how you'll feel if you stay the whole month and then leave, a little voice inside her cried.

While she was still in the throes of turmoil, Nicco returned to the lodge. He seemed in much better spirits than when he'd left. Signora Donatti, a charming woman Callie had taken to at once, didn't have to urge Nicco to eat the home-cooked meal she'd prepared for everyone.

He managed to put away several helpings of her delicious linguini and clams and then ask for more chocolate cheesecake. Obviously he'd worked out a solution to his problem. Callie feared it didn't bode well for her.

"You're still the best cook in Torino, Bianca. I will always consider it a privilege to eat at your table. Now it's growing late. We need to get Valentino home so you and the good doctor can retire for the night."

He focused his gaze on Callie. "If you'll go out to the truck, I'll bring the dog. He can rest his head on your lap."

"All right."

After thanking their hosts, she hurried outside and got situated. It had grown dark in the last hour. Soon Nicco appeared carrying the dog in his arms. He laid him carefully on the seat. Valentino automatically rested his head on top of her thigh where she could hold and protect him.

Dr. Donatti handed her a bottle of painkillers. Callie grabbed his hand and shook it. "Thank you for everything."

He smiled. "You sound like we're never going to see each other again. I expect you to drop by with Valentino in a few days."

"We'll try."

Nicco's lack of commitment made Callie want to break down and sob. It had been such a wonderful day, but it wasn't real. None of it was real because their marriage was based on a lie that was going to blow up in her face before the night was out.

He started up the engine. In a minute they drove away from the lodge without saying anything. They'd been driving for a while before she noticed that they were headed away from the city.

"Where are you going?"

"To the farmhouse."

She blinked in surprise. "Why?"

"Valentino loves it there. He can lie in front of the fire, roam wherever he wants inside or out. The apartment is too cramped. I want him to be comfortable while he's convalescing." After a brief silence, "Do you have a problem with that?"

Her breath caught. "There's only one bedroom."

"We managed before without problem."

"You and I aren't really married—" she blurted.

"We've been over this ground already."

"You know what I mean. The longer we go on with this charade, the more other people are going to get hurt, namely your parents. Their appearance at the surgery has made this all too real."

He pressed harder on the throttle. "If this is your way

of telling me you want out of this marriage early, you can forget it.''

''Please. Just listen to me. I could visit your parents tomorrow and tell them everything. When they understand how far you were willing to go to help your brother, they'll only have cause to love you more than they already do.''

''Have you finished?''

''No! Your parents seem very happy together. They wouldn't want to see you condemned to a loveless marriage. I know they wouldn't!''

He turned in her direction. ''When did you get this sudden, burning desire to go back to California? After I kissed you?'' he demanded.

Even in the semidarkness, he could probably see the red staining her cheeks.

''I thought so,'' he bit out in what sounded like utter disgust. ''If my intention had been to sleep with you, I'd have crawled under the sheets with you that first night like you were daring me to do.''

Her eyes closed tightly remembering what a botch she'd made of that failed ploy.

He geared down to pass another car. ''Never fear. Surely after surviving our honeymoon, you realize you're safe with me. When I want that kind of pleasure, there are women I know who—''

''You've made your point!'' she blurted in fresh agony. Every word from his mouth was like the plunge of a dagger to her heart.

''Now that we have that out of the way, why don't you tell me what my father said to tie you up in little knots.''

Her mouth was so dry, she couldn't swallow. ''He

hoped I would call him Papo by the time we had a baby.''

Nicco burst into deep-bellied laughter. ''Did you tell him we have Valentino who's enough baby for both of us?''

''Laugh all you want, Nicco, but your father meant every word. Both your parents are going to be crushed when they find out we're divorcing. In the beginning you were worried about it, too, so don't try to deny it.''

''Who's denying it? But remember there are no guarantees that two people will stay together, not even when they have the kind of marriage that's based on a deep, abiding love.

''In my parents' case, I've decided to give them credit for being mature adults who will deal with their pain when the time comes. At this point I'm much more concerned about your mental state.''

''Mine?''

''That's right. What's your hurry to be gone? Or is there something you haven't told me...''

When he got that frigid tone, it made her jittery. ''I don't know what you mean.''

''I think you do. Is there a man in your life you've been keeping a secret from me?''

Yes! she cried inwardly. It's *you*, Nicco. Only you.

''Your silence speaks loudly. Who's the man? Dr. Wood?''

''Oh for heaven's sake, no! He was married with children when I was just a little girl.''

''Then it's the guy the who sold you his Strada 100. Jerry, I think you said.''

Nicco had a memory like a computer. She tossed her

head. "This is an absurd conversation. I don't want to talk about it anymore."

"I thought you told me he was married."

"He is!"

"But he still comes to see you every once in a while."

"To see his family!"

"It'll serve him right to learn you're married and living out of the country where you no longer worship at his feet."

"He taught me how to ride, Nicco. That's not something I'll ever forget."

"You're too old a woman to continue nursing a crush you should have outgrown by high school."

His comment caused her mind to reel. Filled with jealousy, she eyed him intently. "You've already passed the third of a century mark. How many girls did *you* teach to ride in your time?"

He slowed down to negotiate the turn onto the farmhouse road. "The only woman who ever got near one of my bikes taught me a lesson I'll never forget."

She felt prickly heat invade her body. "Does that mean you have an extra bike I could ride?"

"Make up your mind if you're staying or leaving."

"For heaven's sake, Nicco! You know I'm not going to do anything that will rebound on your brother."

He pulled up to the farmhouse door and shut off the motor. "I didn't think so, but I had to be sure. Valentino wouldn't understand if you walked away from him now."

"As if I could," she whispered to the beautiful dog who lay there with his eyes half closed.

"Give me a moment to go inside and spread a blanket for him in front of the fire."

When he opened the driver's door, cold mountain air filled the cab. It was a lot nippier than a few nights ago. Her eyes searched the darkness for his tall, powerful silhouette, but he'd disappeared inside the farmhouse.

If he loved her, everything she could ever want was right here. Since he didn't, she would have to pretend he was a friend, nothing more.

"Surely I can handle it for a few more weeks, Valentino. When the pain is unbearable, I'll burden you. How does that sound?"

Deep in thought she let out a small cry of surprise when her door opened. She hadn't heard Nicco's approach.

"Everything's ready. Come on, boy."

The dog lifted his head and tried to get up, but he was pretty unsteady. Nicco caught him in a secure hold and carried him inside the farmhouse. Callie followed with the pills.

The caretaker must have started a grate fire long before they arrived. It crackled and spit, illuminating the two mattresses Nicco had placed on either side of a blanket. Valentino already lay on top of it in front of the hearth.

"Stay with him while I bring everything in from the back of the truck."

She nodded. As soon as he'd gone out, she found a knife in the kitchen drawer and used the end of it to crush one of the pills in a bowl. In the fridge were several bottles of orange juice. She opened one and added a little to the pill which she swirled with her pinky. Next she walked over to the dog and set it by him.

"Come on and drink, Valentino. Your throat hurts, but I know you're thirsty."

As she'd done with the Loti's cat, she dipped her fingers in the liquid, then put them in the dog's mouth. Valentino licked them. When he discovered it was sweet, he drank from the bowl she held for him.

"That's it. Good boy."

Thrilled to see it disappear, she poured in more juice.

Nicco entered the room with his arms full of sacks and put them on the kitchen counter. His gaze darted to the near-empty bottle.

"He's already swallowed his medicine," she was happy to announce.

"You have strong magic," he murmured in a husky tone.

"No. Just common sense. When my tonsils came out, I ate a lot of frozen juice on a stick. A dog is no different."

"If you want to get ready for bed, I'll see that he finishes it."

Pleased to have something new of her own to wear, she left the two of them alone and went into the bedroom with the wardrobe she'd purchased earlier in the day.

After a quick shower she put on a nightgown and robe. When she returned to the fireplace, she noticed Nicco had brought in more firewood. He'd also supplied them with blankets and pillows.

Anxious to be of help, she rinsed out Valentino's bowl and filled it with fresh water for him. When there was nothing else to be done, she got down on the mattress and undid her braid. She started to brush her hair. It felt good.

Soon Nicco joined her. He'd dressed in a clean pair of navy sweats. Between that color and black, she didn't know which looked best on him. His gorgeous olive complexion combined with black hair and eyes set his extraordinary looks apart from other men. She could feast her eyes on him forever.

He lounged on top of his mattress and talked to Valentino in Italian. Whatever he said caused the dog to wag his short tail.

She smiled. "I have to know what you said to him."

Nicco smiled back, turning her heart over and over. "I told him we'd play ball in the courtyard tomorrow. He loves it when I hide it and he has to look for it. I tell him if he's hot or cold."

"Valentino? You're so smart it's scary!"

He made a funny rumbling sound deep in his throat.

While she sat there, she became aware of the horrible itch on her hands she got from scrubbing. It reminded her to pull out the cream Dr. Donatti had suggested she try. She opened the tube and rubbed it into her skin, but she didn't hold out much hope. Still, it had been kind of him to offer a remedy.

She felt Nicco's intense gaze. "Are you allergic to something?"

"Yes. It's the soap I have to use before an operation."

He frowned and sat up. "I noticed the rash on your hands when I put the betrothal ring on you."

"I'll bet you did. Most women have soft, beautiful skin. I'm the furthest thing from the Princess and the Pea you'll ever find. Kind of ironic, isn't it?"

"Most women don't have your gifts."

"Thank you, Nicco. I'll accept that as a compliment."

"It was meant as one."

"Nicco—" She put the cap back on the ointment and pocketed it. "What am I going to do for the next three weeks? Naturally I'll watch after Valentino until he's well, but he'll be healed in a few days. The thing is, I'm used to being busy.''

His eyes narrowed on her features. "For one thing, I planned to take you to work with me.''

Finally! "What is it you do?''

"Why not tell me.''

"After that ironclad contract you drew up, I should imagine you're an attorney.''

"I'm afraid she's cold, Valentino.''

"A seaman then?'' He loved the water.

"Colder still. If you'll be patient for a few more days, then I'll indulge your curiosity.''

"Is it so mysterious you can't tell me now?''

"No. I simply want the satisfaction of watching your reaction.''

"Now I *am* intrigued.''

"Good. Intrigue is the spice of life.''

She cocked one expressive brow. "With those Borgia genes, you come by it naturally.''

Their eyes held in the firelight.

"What happened to my Machiavellian genes?''

"Those, too.''

"You're not nervous of me?''

Nervous.

Excited.

In awe of you.

In love with you.

I'm all of those things.

Callie took a deep breath. "Should I be?''

"Maybe.''

A frisson of delight chased across her skin. "Don't tell me you turn into something else at the stroke of midnight—''

"It might be better if we don't find out," came the cryptic comment.

He got to his feet in one lithe move. With the flames casting shadows, he looked larger than life and infinitely more dangerous than he had at the airport when she'd first seen him.

Valentino wasn't the only one who gazed up at him in worship. Once again he'd caught her making a fool of herself. She turned her head to the side.

"Before it gets any later, I need to talk to the Cozzas."

"Are they the caretakers?"

"That's right. I won't be long. Don't be nervous. I'll lock the door when I go out."

"We'll be fine," she assured him.

After she heard the click, she removed her robe and got under the covers. For the next hour she pondered his strange mood, not able to make sense of it.

Nicco had so many parts that went to make up his fascinating personality, she couldn't keep track of them all. But she wasn't complaining. The only thing that mattered was that he'd become her entire world.

She was here with him now. And here she would stay until he sent her away.

CHAPTER EIGHT

THREE nights later Callie left Nicco and the dog sleeping in front of the hearth. As carefully as possible she tiptoed to the bedroom to phone her boss on Nicco's cell phone. It was two in the morning. Hopefully Dr. Wood would still be at the hospital before he slipped home for dinner.

"North Monterey County Animal Hospital."

"Hi, Janie. It's Callie. How's everything going?"

"Callie! Everything's great, but you just missed Dr. Wood. He's over at the Selanders's."

"You're kidding! That's why I'm calling. I wanted to know if their mare had delivered yet."

"It's happening as we speak."

"I should have been there."

"Instead of being on vacation? Surely you're joking! I would kill to have won a month's vacation to Italy of all places. All those sexy hunks hanging around the piazzas looking even more gorgeous than the statues, if you know what I mean."

Callie clutched the phone until it almost cut into her skin. She knew what Janie meant only too well. By an uncanny quirk of fate, she was married to the most gorgeous one of all. It was time to change the subject.

"How's Chloe?"

"She sleeps in the hall between the surgery and your apartment waiting for you."

"Oh..." Tears filled Callie's eyes.

"Dr. Wood takes her home every night to be with Roxy so she won't be so lonely. He thinks it's helping."

Roxy was an adorable Boston terrier. "That sounds like our Dr. Wood."

"He's a real sweetheart all right."

"Janie? Will you please tell him I called?"

"Of course. I'd put Chloe on the phone, but when you're not here she gets nervous if anyone comes close to her except Dr. Wood."

"I know. Thanks for the thought, Janie."

"You bet. Take my advice and enjoy yourself for as long as you can before you have to come home."

Home?

How would Prunedale ever feel like home again if Nicco weren't there?

Phoning the hospital hadn't been such a good idea after all. Her emotions lay too close to the surface.

"Callie? Are you still there?"

"What? Oh, yes. Of course!" she hastened to assure the receptionist while she wiped her eyes. "It sounds like you've got another call. I'll talk to you again soon. Bye."

She clicked off, terrified at the prospect of leaving Nicco for good. Her world would never be the same again.

Eager to watch him while he slept, she hurried into the other room. After putting the phone on the counter, she crept over to her mattress to lie down again.

"Homesick already?" came the sound of the low, vibrant voice she loved so much.

She quivered. If only he knew the truth...

"I thought I'd better call my boss and check in."

"All is well?"

"Yes." Her heart was pounding so hard, she was certain he could hear it. "I'm sorry if I woke you."

"You didn't. I haven't been able to sleep."

Callie jerked her head in his direction. "Why? Are you sick?"

"No."

"Then what's wrong?" she cried softly in alarm.

"Haven't you noticed?"

She sat up and pushed the hair out of her eyes. "Noticed what? I don't understand."

"Listen—"

Nicco was a grown man, but over the last few days while they'd taken leisurely walks with the dog and had fixed disgustingly fattening meals which they consumed with relish, she discovered he could act just like an incorrigible little boy.

By now Valentino was wide awake. He got up on all fours in his guard stance.

"I don't hear anything."

"*Exactamente!* You've solved Valentino's snoring problem. It used to keep me awake nights. Now the silence is torturing me."

His response was so unexpected, Callie burst into laughter. "You should have thought of that sooner."

"That's not all," he muttered, sounding out of sorts. "He's not my dog anymore. Since you came to live with us, his favorite place to sleep is on your leg. I'm lonely over here all by myself."

So am I, Nicco. I want you so badly, I'm in pain.

"Close your eyes and I'll tell you a story."

"What kind?"

"The only kind. Once upon a time there was this handsome prince who lived in a faraway kingdom."

"My mother tried to read me that fairy tale once," Nicco interrupted, "but I didn't like it."

"That doesn't surprise me. Like you, this prince was blessed with all the riches that could be bestowed on a mere mortal. You wouldn't think he would be sad, would you? But he was.

"He had the run of the forest which of course made him a superb athlete. Over the years he became a friend to the creatures and did all sorts of good deeds, but there was a growing restlessness inside him.

"Every evening before the sun set, he would climb up to his isolated tower and look through the invisible bars of his castle window, wishing he could be free like the townspeople below."

Valentino decided to lie down again. At least Callie's bedtime story appeared to be putting *him* to sleep.

"Ironically those very townspeople who lived in the valley were busy dreaming their own dreams. They would look out the windows of their cramped apartments. Beyond the noise, beyond the wash hanging on the line, they would gaze longingly at the castle on the hill, wishing they could be the prince and ride around the country all day in his chauffeur-driven royal limousine while they ate chocolates."

"Chocolates?" His bark of laughter reverberated off the walls of the cozy room.

Her mouth curved upward. "Hand-dipped truffles and succulent golden pears from the royal fruit trees growing outside the prince's window."

After his laughter subsided he said, "I don't believe the prince had any idea such thoughts were going on inside the heads of the townspeople."

She remained poker-faced. "Well, he wouldn't, would

he. Not when all his energy was devoted to gaining his freedom.''

''In order to do what?''

''Ah… I thought you didn't like fairy tales.''

''I've changed my mind.''

''Unfortunately I don't know the rest.''

''Don't leave me hanging now,'' he said in a strangely thick voice. ''You were just getting to the good part. Make it up if you have to. Live dangerously.''

Callie sent him a covert glance. When she discovered his gleaming black eyes trained on her in the dying light of the embers, her body trembled.

''I thought that's what I was doing by staying here with you.''

He raked a hand through his luxuriant black hair as if he were disturbed by something. ''I tell you what. Tomorrow I'll show you what happened to the prince so you'll know the end of the story.''

Though she was jumping out of her skin with excitement, she merely nodded. ''That would be nice. Now I don't know about you, but I've managed to make myself sleepy.''

No sooner had she put her head back down than she felt him move around to her other side.

''Nicco?'' she cried in an unsteady voice. He'd drawn close to her the way he'd done the first night at the farmhouse. ''What are you doing?''

He buried his face in the profusion of her newly washed hair. ''You don't mind if I hold on to you, do you? I'm cold.''

The exact words she'd used on him when she'd had the ridiculous idea to tempt him into kissing her.

''I-isn't there any more firewood outside?''

''Not unless I chop it.'' He slid his arm around her to get comfortable.

She waited for what seemed like a long time, expecting his lips to make a foray to hers. Hungry, desperate for his mouth, she finally turned a little to help him. Ever since that moment before his parents had interrupted them in the surgery, she'd been longing to be in his arms again.

Feverish for contact she whispered, ''Nicco?''

There was no answer.

She lifted her head and discovered he'd fallen asleep. For the rest of the night she lay there in agony, sandwiched between the man and dog she adored.

Positive she would stay wide-awake for the rest of the night, it surprised her that she didn't stir again until mid-morning. To her profound disappointment, she found herself alone.

Nicco had left her a note on the kitchen counter.

I've taken Valentino to the Cozzas. When I return, we'll ride into Torino. It's brisk out. Since we're going on the bike, better wear the sweater you bought.

Her disappointment changed to excitement. At last she was going to find out what this complicated former prince did to earn his daily bread. Whatever it was, he was probably thrilled to have the whole wedding business behind him so he could get back to his normal routine. Far be it from her to keep him from his work.

After a quick breakfast, she hurriedly braided her hair. Before she left the bathroom, she applied a new apricot frost lipstick. Until now she'd worn no makeup at all.

She eyed her purchases sitting on the bed. After a moment she chose to dress in the new cream-colored jeans and a matching long-sleeved turtleneck. They toned nicely with her new tan cardigan and sandals.

When Nicco breezed in the farmhouse door minutes later declaring he was ready to go, he didn't say anything about her appearance. However as he donned his motorcycle jacket, his black eyes seemed to linger on her face and figure longer than usual, dissolving her bones with that look.

She put on her helmet, pretending a nonchalance she didn't feel before following him out the door. He'd already wheeled his bike from the garage into the courtyard.

Callie walked over to it. "In the sun your motorcycle looks like an enticing lick of red flame. It has so much personality it says 'I'm here. Take me if you dare.'"

"As I recall, you already did that."

Their eyes caught after he'd fastened the chin strap of his helmet.

"I'm sorry for that, Nicco."

"Don't ruin it," he mocked. "Given enough provocation, you and I both know you'd do it again without the slightest hesitation. I've lived with you long enough to know we're two of a kind." He got on the bike to start it.

Two of a kind?

She flung her leg over the seat and grabbed him around his taut stomach. "I'll have you know I descend from the Vikings!"

Laughter escaped. "I thought as much the first time I laid eyes on you at the airport. You're a lot of woman, *esposa mia*. Most men would be terrified to take you on."

Her retort was lost in the scream of the motor. By the

time they reached the highway, any leftover rage was swallowed up in the utter joy of being with this man she loved to the depth of her soul.

This time when they reached the outskirts of Torino, he headed in an easterly direction. Once they left the freeway he took a series of turns until they came to an area that looked industrialized rather than residential.

He eventually slowed down to negotiate a turn into the parking area of a compound of warehouses. She saw dozens of cars. There was one small office building. Nicco didn't stop until he'd pulled around the back of it. After they jumped off the bike, he used a key to let them inside a door bearing a sign in Italian that she assumed meant "private."

He led her to the first door on their left. It looked like a normal office equipped with computers and monitors.

While he went over to his desk, she removed her helmet. "Do you own your own computer business or something?" she asked after turning to face him.

Nicco had discarded his helmet and jacket. Now he was seated in his swivel chair booting up his main computer. She got the impression he hadn't heard her question. At closer inspection she realized a fire burned within him. Its energy reached out to her like a living thing, compelling her to move around and see what he was seeing.

A design labeled Prototype I, Danelli NT-1 super racing bike, came up on the screen. Another click of the mouse and an enlargement of the intricate engine design sprang before her eyes. It set off a chain reaction in her head.

"NT... Nicco Tescotti," she whispered in awe as all the pieces of the puzzle began to fit into place.

He was a mechanical engineer.

"You've replaced Ernesto Strada..." That's how Nicco had access to certain information the rest of the motorcycle world didn't know.

He shook his head. "I could never fill the shoes of such a genius. The round piston, dual ignition, the single side arm—all those were his inventions. He was a man far ahead of his time. Except for Luca who had family money, most of the people in the business thought he was crazy."

"Like a fox," Callie murmured. "My Strada 100 still puts the competition to shame."

Nicco nodded. "I've just refined his ideas a little more using EDF digital modeling. Now everything's fully fuel injected. Luca happened to like those changes. One thing led to another. He decided to put Danelli bikes back on the map and brought me along for the ride."

"Don't be so modest, Nicco. Please show me what else you've designed."

He typed in something else. While they waited for it to appear he said, "The motorcycles you're about to see are for the road, not for racing competition. Except for contacting a few major distributors in Europe, I've done the majority of marketing over the Internet."

"I bet orders are flooding in from around the world."

He nodded. "It's a shame the Internet wasn't available to Ernesto. Here's one of our most popular models. It's the 600 cc, specially designed for comfort during long trips. More and more women are riding these days. I intended it to appeal to the fairer sex, but men seem to like it, too."

One by one they flashed on the screen: café au lait

and chocolate, aqua and cobalt blue, tangerine and cream, purple and lavender.

"Ooh... I wouldn't know which one to pick!" she cried excitedly. "They're all so beautiful."

"I've named this model *La Dolce Vita.*"

"The good life." She read the translation out loud. "It's the perfect name for it. With that chocolate one, you've tapped into the secret delight of the general public."

Nicco grinned.

"And here I thought the poor prince didn't have a clue. No wonder they're selling like hotcakes. Show me more."

She heard the click of the mouse and yet another model appeared on the screen.

"This one is the 1000 cc, fully loaded to appeal to the racing driver who still wants something powerful when he's not on the bike he uses at the track. It comes in a range of the primary colors with black."

Callie leaned closer. 'You've named it *The Sidewinder.* Where I come from, that's a rattlesnake."

"You go to the head of the class. The snake moves by a distinctive lateral looping motion of its body and delivers a powerful punch from the side. Exactly what the rider wants on crowded mountain passes."

"Let me see all of them!"

For the next little while he kept her enthralled.

"Don't tell me that's it?" she cried when he'd finished with the series.

"The rest are racing bikes."

"Like your red one?"

"Yes."

"What do you call yours?"

"The Monster."

"How appropriate!"

He chuckled.

"Okay, Nicco Tescotti. Confess. Now I want to see your secret weapon for the female professional racer."

One black brow quirked rather diabolically. "You think I have one?"

"I *know* you do."

In a surprise move he turned off the computer and got to his feet. When she looked into his black eyes, they were alive with passion. But it was a passion reserved for his work.

If ever he were to look at you like that, Callie Lassiter...

"Such faith deserves a reward," he murmured.

Euphoric at this point, she followed him out the door and down the hall to a back room. When he unlocked it and ushered her inside, she let out a gasp.

Propped in the middle of a room surrounded by racing gear was a bike like nothing she'd ever seen. Dazzled by the tricolored motorcycle in silver and gold with thin strippings of cream to stylize it, she was at a loss for words.

"You like it?"

"Like it—" she squealed the words before approaching it with reverence. "How can you even ask me that question? I've never seen anything so stunning in my life. Talk about a secret weapon!

"If you were to allow it on the track, there would be dozens of accidents because the other drivers would take one look at it and forget what they were supposed to be doing."

"I agree."

His voice sounded so husky she lifted her head to glance at him, only to discover his gaze leveled on her with an intensity that held her spellbound.

"I—I would imagine Lancelot made this same kind of impact when he galloped beneath the sun in full, gleaming armor."

A ghost of a smile hovered around Nicco's lips. "Actually I had Lady Godiva in mind. The glint of the sun of her long gossamer hair. Rather breathtaking."

"You mean when the wind came along. So *that's* what the prince was dreaming about from his tower window," she teased.

He flashed her a wicked smile. "Something like that."

She went weak in the knees. "What did you name this one?"

"I haven't decided yet. It's down to two choices."

"So you're not going to tell me?"

"I'm afraid not. This racing model isn't for sale yet."

"Why?"

"I've tested it on the track, but not the road. In the end, it's still the long haul that counts."

Callie turned her back on the bike. "I almost wish I hadn't seen it."

His brows furrowed. "Why?"

"Thou Shalt Not Covet."

Nicco broke into rich male laughter, the kind she loved to hear.

"It's not funny, Nicco. When I go home I shall have to be happy with my Strada 100." She bit her lip. "Of course I *am* happy with it. But you know what I mean. Thank you for bringing me to your work. I've had the time of my life. Now I think you'd better take me back to the farmhouse. Valentino will be expecting to go for a walk.''

"You don't want a tour of the factory first?"

"No. I'd better not. As my mother used to tell me, if you can't afford it, then don't go window shopping."

"Your mother sounds like a wise woman."

"She was. If she'd lived below the prince's castle, she would have looked up once, then never again."

"That kind of self-discipline is rare."

"I know. My sister got so frustrated, she made certain she *could* afford it. I'm beginning to think she was right. On a vet's pay, I might be able to afford such a luxury after about thirty years of saving. By that time I'll be too old and fat to straddle one," she grumbled.

"Well if that's in your future, then you'd better take advantage of my offer now."

Her head came up. "What offer?"

"Ever since I watched the expert way you stole my bike out from under me and took off, I've had this urge to take you on a road trip with me."

She blinked. "You're kidding. Aren't you?"

"Here—let's get you properly outfitted."

He moved so fast pulling things off shelves, she couldn't keep up with him. Soon she was feasting her eyes on a gleaming, cream-colored helmet with matching leather Kevlar gloves, boots, pants and jacket.

He helped her on with everything, then zipped her up. Where his fingers touched, she felt as if she'd been scorched.

"Nicco—I didn't even know they made leather motorcycle accessories this color!"

"Everything was specially ordered to go with the bike."

For a moment the world stood still.

"You're going to let me ride *this* one?"

Their eyes fused. "Why not?"

"But, Nicco—"

"No buts. Where's the fiery daredevil who planned her successful getaway the second she laid eyes on my bike?"

Callie blushed before spinning around to look at it again. Then she stared back at him. "What if something happens and I cra—"

"God willing, we'll both return safe and sound," he broke in on her. "Come. I'll walk it outside. You can drive it around the parking lot for a few minutes to get used to it before we head out."

She could hardly breathe for the joy that news brought her. "Where are we going to go on our trip?"

"Now that I know your penchant for chocolate, I thought we'd ride to Switzerland!" he called over his shoulder.

Running after him in a state of total exhilaration she cried, "I've always wanted to go there!"

In a few minutes she was driving around on the magnificent machine, incredulous that this was happening to her. To think all those years growing up she'd sat inside Jerry's garage next door dreaming about riding on a fabulous Danelli...

Nicco had gone inside the office for his gear. Now everything was locked and he was back, ready to roll. He watched her pull up next to him.

Lifting his shield he said, "What do you think, Signora Tescotti?"

"If Jerry could see me now, he wouldn't believe it.

Oh, Nicco—this is the most exciting day of my whole life! There are no words to thank you for—''

But before she could finish telling him of her gratitude, he'd fired up his bike. The next thing she knew he'd pulled away from her. In a matter of seconds he was a red blur in the distance.

What on earth?

Why had he driven off like that without giving her any warning?

Something had gotten into him to leave her behind. What worried her was that she feared he might not wait for her when he discovered she couldn't keep up.

If she were on the Strada, that would be one thing. Instead she was astride the greatest racing bike in the world! A bike she didn't own and could never pay for in several lifetimes.

Maybe he was testing her to see if *she* was roadworthy. It was something those Machiavellian genes would think up. In that case, she would just have to show him what she was made of and pray nothing happened to his bike.

Heads turned to stare as she whizzed faster and faster past cars and pedestrians. A couple of guys on Vespas whistled and tried in vain to catch up to her. She increased her speed to stay within sight of her moving red target, determined that Nicco wouldn't lose her no matter how hard he tried.

The chase was on.

Her bike was so powerful, it gobbled up the kilometers. In no time at all they'd left Torino and had climbed into the mountains. The sun played peekaboo behind clouds that were forming the farther north they flew.

Traffic was moderate enough she could swing from

lane to lane without having to change gears. Nicco must have decided to take pity on her because the next time she rounded a curve on the mountain road, he pulled next to her.

When she chanced a look at him, he gave her the thumbs-up. Coming from him, that was great praise. Relief washed over her in waves that he seemed himself again. Now she could relish the scenery in earnest.

Callie had only seen Lake Maggiore in picture books. It was hard to believe that the next vista opening up to her hungry eyes revealed the famous jewellike lake dotted with picturesque chalets clustered along its shoreline.

Between the combination of Nicco riding next to her and the breathtaking sight, she was positive she'd been transported to another dimension of joy.

After the road dropped down into the valley, she followed Nicco's lead and got off at the next exit. Then it was a race to catch up with him again as he found another road that wound away from the lake and up into the high mountain pastures.

Here there was no traffic to speak of. They could lean into the curves and ride like the wind while they continued their journey north. Though thunderheads were beginning to form, Nicco appeared oblivious.

Like happy children let out to play, they basked in their freedom to go where they wanted and thrill to the magic of it all.

Everything would have been perfect if it hadn't started to rain. At first it came down in random drops. Soon there were gusts of wind that pelted them against her face guard.

Nicco waved to her to follow him. They started down the mountain toward the town she'd seen at the north end of the lake. Probably for her sake he didn't drive as fast as he would have if he'd been alone. For that she was grateful. Once the road was wet, the tires didn't grip the surface the same way.

When they finally reached Locarno where she could see the Swiss flag emblazoned on shutters outside one of the hotels, they'd arrived in the middle of a drenching downpour.

Thank goodness Nicco knew where to go. In a minute he'd found them a service station where they could park under the overhang and fill up their gas tanks.

After paying the attendant, Nicco came back outside to join her. Until they'd stopped riding, she hadn't noticed how cold it was.

"I've heard this storm won't blow out before morning. I phoned a guesthouse not far from here I've used before. They have a vacancy. Let's go."

Callie's heart skipped a beat.

Since she'd arrived in Italy they'd been sharing quarters at the apartment, on the barge and at the farmhouse. Having to stay in the same room with him tonight shouldn't be any different.

But somehow it *was*.

Tonight she wouldn't have Valentino to use as a shield.

CHAPTER NINE

"HERE we are. *Affettato musto, cazzola, nocino and torte della nonna.*"

The ruddy-cheeked Swiss woman who ran the guest-house with her husband brought dinner to their room and put it on the table near the fireplace. "Enjoy your meal," she said in English with a heavy Ticino accent.

"*Grazie.*" Nicco shut the door after her.

A fire blazed in the hearth. With the rain still pounding against the roof of the chalet, the scene couldn't have been cozier. *Or more romantic.*

Haunted by that aspect, Callie sent Nicco surreptitious glances as he closed the distance between them to join her. In a black turtleneck and jeans, his masculine appeal overwhelmed her.

He's my husband by law as well as the law of the church. He's the husband of my heart. Yet what am I to him?

"E-everything sounds so special when you say it in Italian," she stammered. "What is *affettato?*"

"Nothing terribly exciting."

For the first time in her presence, he sounded bored. Nicco could have no idea how much it hurt.

"It's an antipasto of salami and hams. For the main course, various sausages with potatoes and cheese. Dessert is a sugar tart I guarantee you'll enjoy. The *nocino* I'm not sure about where you're concerned."

"*Nocino?*"

"Um...a spicy walnut-flavored grappa liqueur. It's excellent at the end of a meal following a cup of coffee."

"I'll have to try it later."

"Our ride seems to have brought out your more adventurous side."

He was acting so strange again. His mercurial mood told her something was definitely wrong. She began to eat, but the silence between them dragged on. Halfway through their meal, she couldn't take it any longer.

"I'll never forget today, Nicco. I started to thank you in front of your office building, but you rode off before I could finish."

He ate the last of the potatoes and onions. "You don't have to thank me. I told you that if you would cooperate at the marriage ceremony, you could pick out any bike you liked for a wedding present. I always keep my promises."

Callie lowered her head. Tonight she was seeing a side of him that was foreign to her.

Don't be like this, Nicco. You're acting so cold and aloof.

She put down her fork, unable to indulge an appetite that had fled. "I couldn't possibly keep the bike."

"Why is that?" he inquired civilly. "Because your strange code of honor won't allow you to accept my gift unless we've slept together first? If that's what is holding you back, we can remedy the situation tonight."

Her breathing grew shallow. "Don't make light of something that's sacred to me."

"You mean you intend to go to your death still saving yourself for Jerry what's-his-name?"

She needed to get beyond his baiting.

"There was a time when I made a fool of myself around him, but he was eight years older than I, and always treated me like a pesky kid. We remained friends because of our love of cycling. Period."

"He was still on your mind today," Nicco persisted before swallowing a tart whole.

She pushed herself away from the table and stood up. "He *would* be since he owned a Danelli and introduced me to the sport. If he had any idea I had been riding around in the Alps on the latest racing creation of Danelli's chief engineer, he'd have a coronary. In fact, he wouldn't believe me."

"Does he still race?"

"No. Now that they have children, his wife made him give it up."

"The poor devil," he muttered under his breath, but she heard him. It caused another wrench to her heart.

"Not every man wants his freedom as much as you do, Nicco. I promise I'll be out of your hair the second the thirty days are up." She started for the door.

"Where do you think you're going?"

"Downstairs. I saw some maps and postcards at the front desk I'd like to buy."

"I'll come with you."

"No—" she blurted. "Please—stay and enjoy your coffee."

He rose to his feet. "I'd rather accompany my wife than drink alone."

Callie hesitated before opening the door. "Please don't refer to me in that light."

His expression hardened. "What light is that? For better or worse, you *are* my wife. Whether you accept that fact or not, the bike is yours."

They were back to that again.

Feeling weak, she braced herself against the door-jamb. "I've done nothing to deserve it. You had to drag me to the church."

"True." He came closer. "However you could have made a scene in front of the priest, and you didn't. For that you not only have *my* gratitude, but Enzo's."

"That still doesn't mean you owe me something worth $150,000. If anyone should understand, *you* should."

He regarded her with those black, impenetrable eyes, daring her to go on.

"I would imagine one of the reasons you renounced the throne was because you didn't feel entitled to all the land and wealth you didn't earn by the sweat of your own brow. I respect you more than you know for acting on your principles."

"I admit that was part of it, but not all."

Nicco was still holding back. Since he didn't feel inclined to share the rest with her, there wasn't anything more to say. Wishing the pain would go away, she darted out the door.

"Prince Tescotti— Princess—give us a look!"

Unprepared for a barrage of camera flashes, she recoiled straight into Nicco chest. He pulled her back into the room. Once he'd slammed the door, he moved her against it until there was no space between them.

"I was afraid the paparazzi might be lurking out there. That's why I didn't want you to go downstairs alone."

Her face was buried in his neck. "They surprised me, that's all. I should have remembered how much you hate the press and stayed put for your sake."

"Forget me, Callie. You're the one who needs protection. Until you return to California, I think we'll remain at the farmhouse where you can enjoy your freedom in relative privacy.''

She closed her eyes tightly. He couldn't have made it any clearer that there would be a divorce in the near future. Like a lovesick idiot, her subconscious had been living in denial.

Not anymore!

With those words he'd just given her the kind of wake-up call she couldn't afford to ignore. In order to survive until she left Italy, there was only one thing to do.

''I think I'm ready to try that liqueur.'' As she eased away from his arms, their bodies produced breathtaking friction. ''Shall I pour you a drink?'' Somehow she made it over to the table without collapsing.

He followed, but there was no answer to her question. That was all right. She'd do it anyway. When she'd filled the liqueur glasses, she lifted them and handed one to him. Girding up her courage, she met his jet black gaze without flinching.

''Before I ask an important favor of you, I'd like to make a toast. To *you,* Nicco. You're not the wolf in prince's clothing I accused you of being when my sister begged me to bail her out of a horrendous situation.''

She touched his glass with hers, then drank the dark liquid in one swallow. It burned all the way down her throat. But she was already in agony, so she scarcely felt the pain.

Nicco didn't make a move to swallow his. In fact there was an ominous stillness about him that was very unnerving.

''Now for the favor,'' she continued on. ''Would you

be kind enough to ask Dr. Donatti if I could spend time at his surgery until you and I part company? You need to get back to your work, and I need to stay busy. Because the hospital is located on a wooded estate, Dr. Donatti sees a lot of wildlife I don't. If he wouldn't mind, I could learn a lot just watching him.''

Nicco chose that moment to empty the contents of his glass. ''You wouldn't be able to stay there nights,'' he declared rather aggressively after setting it down.

''Of course not. That would defeat the whole purpose of your elaborate plan. I thought you could drive me to the lodge when you're ready for work, then pick me up at the end of the day. We'd maintain the illusion of a normal married couple.''

An inscrutable expression broke out on his face. He seemed to be pondering something weighty in his mind because she noticed how he rubbed his chest in an unconscious gesture.

''If it would make you happy, I'll talk to him.''

That had gone easier than she'd thought. No doubt Nicco had been wondering what to do with her for the three remaining weeks. After her welcome suggestion, he could relax.

''I would appreciate it. Thank you.'' She put her glass on the table. ''Unless you'd prefer to go first, I'd like to shower.''

He gave an almost imperceptible nod of his dark head. ''I'm in no hurry. The favor I intend to extract from you can wait until later.''

Those last words set off alarm bells. Adrenaline shot through her veins as she scrambled for the bathroom. When she came out later dressed in one of the robes the guesthouse provided, he was sitting at the table talking on the phone. Someone had been to the room to clear away the remains of their dinner.

Troubled by his all-encompassing gaze, she scurried to the bed and climbed under the covers.

"Oh—" she cried softly when she saw a chocolate truffle bar on the pillow she'd uncovered. Delighted by her find, her eyes swiveled to his. "That was very thoughtful. Thank you, Nicco."

"Anything to please my wife."

The blood pounded in her ears. He was sweetening her up for something.

"W-what favor did you want to ask of me?"

"While I was watching the expert way you handled the bike today, several ideas came to me I can't put out of my mind."

She shook her head. "We both know I'm a hopeless amateur."

"You may not have made racing your career, but you're loaded with the kind of natural talent most want-to-bes would kill for. I'm in a position to know, so trust me."

I do. Your praise has already gone to my head like the strong liqueur I drank a little while ago.

She'd been clutching the bar so hard, she'd made the end of it soft. Quickly she put it down on top of the covers. "All I seem to be doing tonight is thanking you."

"You don't hear me complaining, do you?"

"No. Of course not."

He rose to his full intimidating height. "For some time I've been pestered by various editors of cycling magazines around the world to let them do an article. Luca has been pushing me as well."

"I understand why you haven't." Her voice shook. "Trust *me* on that one."

His eyes narrowed on her features. "If I didn't, I wouldn't have let you near the bike that I sense in my gut is going to make Luca's fortune all over again. Little did you know your words were prophetic when you called it a secret weapon."

"I knew," she defended quietly, capturing his gaze. "That bike is revolutionary. It must be galling for you to realize that the only thing those editors really want is the exclusive story about the man who didn't want to be prince. They know it will sell millions of copies. What fools they are not to understand that you'll never give them what they want."

"Not that story certainly," he concurred. "But with your help, I can promote our new product line without bringing my past into it."

My help?

How many times had Callie fought Nicco, only to cave in because she was too in love with him to do anything that would separate her from him. If she didn't stop this madness now, she would be in pain for the rest of her life. Look what had happened because she'd listened to Ann!

This film is going to launch my career, Callie. That's why you have to help me out.

"I'm afraid helping you market your new line of motorcycles falls outside the parameters of the original marriage contract, Nicco."

If she sounded spiteful and immature, so be it. Callie was fighting for a tiny piece of her soul—*if* there was one left which she strongly doubted.

"No problem," he replied unruffled. "What I had in

mind will occur after I accompany you back to the States.''

His declaration gave her her first inkling that maybe he was having as difficult a time as she was at the thought of separation. If that was the case, she was going to make him say the words.

''W-why would you do that?''

''To get a picture of you zooming around a farmer's field on the Strada 100 with your medical bag and your braid flying. That image of you has crystallized certain ideas for an article which has been floating around in my brain. At last I know how to proceed.''

Dear God. And here she'd thought...

''So that's the favor? To pose on my bike for you?''

One black brow gave a sardonic lift. ''While you're making your rounds, the cameraman will shoot pictures. You'll never know he's there.''

Her eyes smarted. She looked away.

Why couldn't you have loved me, Nicco?

''For several years now I've wanted to honor Ernesto and Luca in an innovative way, taking them through the war years to today. The essence of the article will be to show their impact not only on the motorcycle racing world, but on society in general. A picture of a modern-day American vet on one of Ernesto's old models will reinforce the idea that they're built to last forever.

''Your coming to Italy in the place of your sister must have been fate. I'll know the right photo when I see it.''

Recovering as fast as she could she said, ''You mean the one where the bike and I are covered in mud.''

''Something like that.'' The amusement in his eyes was like another fiery salvo to her heart which was bleeding profusely. ''The caption will read, 'Even a mad vet from Prunedale, California, U.S.A., can't do without her Strada 100.'''

Callie lowered her head. She had to admit his idea was pure genius.

There'd been a blanket of secrecy surrounding the shutdown of the Danelli factory. Whichever cycling magazine was given the honor of publishing the news of its spectacular comeback would be making their own fortune on that particular issue.

She was about to say that Jerry would go into cardiac arrest when he discovered the bike he'd sold her had appeared on the front cover. But remembering Nicco's reaction the last time her neighbor's name was mentioned, she thought the better of it.

"There's no question I'm a huge Danelli-Strada fan, so I tell you what—" She raised her head to eye him directly.

"After I'm back home, the cameraman can contact me at the hospital and we'll go from there. Your presence won't be needed. Like you, I always keep my promises."

"I'm glad to hear it, but there won't be an exclusive unless I oversee every aspect of the article including the shoots. In any event, you'll still be my wife."

"What on earth are you talking about?" she cried. "I distinctly remember the marriage contract stating that after thirty days either party could get a divorce, no questions asked."

"Your memory is excellent," he said in a patronizing tone. "However it didn't state how long it would take for the divorce to be granted. That's up to one of our Italian judges to decide."

"Surely the Tescotti name will ensure a swift resolution."

"One can hope."

She gritted her teeth. "What are you implying?"

"Only that our courts are backed up. Until it's official, you'll continue to be my responsibility."

"Don't worry, Nicco. With an ocean between us, you'll be able to carry on as if our marriage had never taken place." *As for me, I have absolutely no idea how I'm going to survive.*

"If I weren't a former prince, I'd do just that. But there's a protocol every Tescotti husband must follow. Until a decree of divorcement is handed down, you're automatically granted my physical protection."

"I don't need it," she bit out in a withering tone.

He looked at her through shuttered eyes. "Nevertheless, I refuse to be the only Tescotti to shirk his marital obligation. So it appears you and I will be living together in California until our marriage is dissolved."

"But that's crazy!"

"Nevertheless that's the way things are." His hands had gone to his hips in a purely male stance. He was so desirable to her, she couldn't think straight around him. "I had the impression you couldn't wait to see Chloe and get back to your practice."

"I can't!" she replied honestly. Every second spent in his company at this point was killing her. If he followed her home...

"What happened to the business about the piece of gossip you were going to give the press? The one about the heartbroken prince whose wife left him because of irreconcilable differences to do with their nationalities?"

"That plan hasn't changed. As soon as my parents

see it, they'll try to reach me. Enzo will tell them I've followed you to Prunedale to try to salvage our marriage.''

By now she was terrified. "You can't just leave your job!"

"The laptop is a great invention. While you're otherwise occupied with your vet duties, I'll work."

She was desperate to find a way out of this new crisis. "The room behind the hospital isn't big enough for two people."

"My barge was smaller."

The barge...

"Valentino will be devastated when you leave."

"He's happy enough at the farmhouse with the Cozzas when I have to be away."

She clutched the covers in a death grip. "Nicco—I don't want you there."

"I know you don't." His voice grated. "Just remember it was love for my brother that produced this situation in the first place. If I'm not mistaken, it was love for your sister that consigned you to your fate. A little patience and this game will play itself out."

"It's a terrible game." Her voice shook.

"Perhaps now you're beginning to understand a portion of the prince's burden as he looked out his tower window."

Her breath caught. "A portion— What's the rest?"

He ignored her and reached for the other robe. "After I've showered, I'll sleep on the couch."

She sat up. "Why won't you answer me?"

"It isn't anything for you to worry about." His inscrutable expression left her the slightest bit uneasy.

"You've just said the very thing guaranteed to make

anyone worry. Nicco? Is there something wrong with you?''

He slowed his steps to the bathroom. ''Is it the doctor in you asking that question?''

''Maybe. The thought just occurred to me that maybe you had another reason for refusing the throne, one your parents don't know about yet.''

''And what would that be pray tell?'' he mocked.

''A degenerating illness perhaps? One which decided you against marriage so you wouldn't bring unbearable pain to the woman you loved.''

''That's an interesting theory. If it were the case, why would it matter to you?''

''I *am* a human being,'' she said in an uneven voice. ''Under such circumstances, no one should be alone.''

''I'm not alone right now.''

''Don't tease about this! I'm talking about a companion who will always be there for you.''

''Are you saying that you're willing to take on the job?''

Staggered by excruciating pain at the very thought of him suffering she blurted, ''Tell me the truth! Do you have an illness?''

''I'm afraid we all have to face death at some point.''

Compelled by a force beyond her control, she slid out of bed and ran over to him. Her hands gripped his strong upper arms. ''Please don't put up a front with me, Nicco. I can't bear it.''

''I had no idea you cared this much,'' he murmured.

''Stop it!''

''Stop what?''

''Don't mock everything I say. For once in your life be serious with me.''

There was a sharp intake of breath. "Is this serious enough for you?" Even as he asked the question, his head descended and he covered her mouth with his own, drawing the very breath from her trembling body.

Starved for his kiss, she wrapped her arms around his neck, loving the freedom to get as close to him as possible.

"Callie—" she heard him cry as he drew her against his hard-muscled physique. With a palpable hunger that seemed to match hers, he swept her away to a place she'd never been before, not even in her dreams.

Somehow they'd graduated to the bed. Tangled in his arms and legs, she pulled his head back down, offering him everything she had to give, wanting this ecstasy to go on and on.

This was rapture beyond comprehension. When he finally released her mouth enough for her to breathe again, she groaned in protest.

"Don't stop, Nicco. I'm here for you. You don't have to worry about being alone."

He buried his face in her neck. "Would you go so far as to have my baby?"

"If it would bring you happiness, then yes," she whispered without hesitation. *Oh, yes.*

His mouth roved over her face, kissing her eyelids, her nose, her avid mouth. "You're an extraordinary woman."

I'm a woman in love, Nicco.

"I wonder if your answer would be the same if you knew my problem wasn't going to lead to an early death."

It took a moment for his comment to penetrate her

brain. Still caught in the throes of passion, she was slow to react.

"You mean you don't have an incurable disease or anything close to it." *How could she have been so stupid as to let this happen? Now he could be in no doubt how much she loved him.*

Pushing him away with all her strength, she jumped off the bed.

He sprang to his feet. "I never said I did."

She fastened the belt of her robe tighter. "No. You simply let me go on assuming as much."

His white smile was too much. "I couldn't help it. I've never known anyone with such a strong sense of self-sacrifice. I'm beginning to understand how your sister was able to manipulate you into coming in her place."

"Damn you, Nicco," she whispered out of lips swollen by his kisses.

"Are you really going to tell me you didn't find our experience as delightful as I did?"

Callie swung the other way, needing to do something with her chaotic emotions. She searched the covers for her chocolate bar.

"Brief as it was, it exceeded all my expectations," he murmured. "In fact I was so enthralled, I came painfully close to forgetting you were prepared to give me a child out of pity rather than love."

"You've made your point, Nicco!" she snapped before biting into a section.

"I must confess that in your arms just now, there came a moment when it was difficult to tell the difference," he persisted in torturing her.

Before she could countenance it, his arms reached

around her from behind. He lifted the bar she was still holding and took a bite.

"Um. That tastes almost as luscious as you do." He planted another seductive kiss on the side of her neck before disappearing into the bathroom.

Tears poured down her cheeks unchecked.

I'll never let you make a fool of me again, Nicco.

While he was in the shower, she found Nicco's cell phone and made a credit card call to Ann who would just be getting up.

Half a dozen Italian news reporters were stuffed inside Nicco's small apartment, filling it to maximum capacity. Valentino walked back and forth in front of the couch where Callie sat next to Nicco whose arm held her firmly around the shoulders.

By tacit agreement they'd both dressed for this interview in the clothes they'd been wearing to work. They consisted of jeans and pullovers.

Nicco acted the devoted husband in front of other people. He knew better than to play the passionate lover.

Since that ghastly experience in Locarno, there'd been no more physical contact except for now, and of course on the back of his bike. No more talks about magazine articles. Nothing about the future. She'd told him a visit to his parents was out of the question.

One week to go and she'd be back in California with Nicco. She couldn't wait for the surprise she had in store for him. Until then she would leave the direction of this interview in his hands. It was vital they protect Enzo.

"Why don't each of you ask a question in turn, starting with you," Nicco suggested. He nodded to the man on the end chair.

The reporter cleared his throat. ''Everyone wants to know how you two met.''

''My brother saw her first while he was on a recent visit to the United States. Upon his return, he showed me her picture. When I remarked on her attractiveness, he told me she was coming to Italy with every intention of buying a motorcycle. Would I help out?

''Since I design them for a living, naturally I told him I'd be only too happy to oblige. She expected to see my brother at the airport. Instead she got me. I've been her captive ever since.''

Nicco was so good it was terrifying.

The next reporter was a woman. She smiled at Callie. ''What did you think when you first met the former prince?''

''That he was dark and dangerous. I found out my instincts were right the moment he kidnapped me on his motorcycle.''

''But you didn't really mind,'' said the third reporter.

''He redeemed himself to some extent when I realized he could ride as well as design a bike. Cycling is one of my hobbies.''

''What actually made you decide on marrying him so soon after meeting him?''

Nicco had been caressing the back of her neck, but the last question caused his hand to still on her heated flesh.

''Valentino.''

At the mention of his name, the dog plopped his head on her knee. She scratched behind his ears. ''This gorgeous fellow stole my heart.''

''My wife's a veterinarian with a thriving practice

back in California,'' Nicco confided, squeezing her neck gently.

Callie cupped the dog's jowls. "With those adoring eyes, who could resist you?"

"How will you handle your marriage when you both have careers on two continents?"

Another round of questions had started. Nicco took the initiative.

"We're still on our honeymoon and haven't ironed everything out yet."

That was the understatement of a lifetime.

The only woman journalist spoke up once more. "How does it feel to be married to a prince?"

Callie took a deep breath. "If we'd married before Nicco renounced his title, I might be able to answer that question. As it is, I can only tell you how it feels to be married to a man who works eight to six at his office.

"We have to adhere to a strict budget because any money Nicco makes he puts back in the company. He's teaching me how to cook and we both take care of Valentino. If there's any free time, we ride our bikes."

The same woman leaned forward with a twinkle in her eye. "What's he really like?" Callie couldn't help but like her.

"His sense of humor can be infuriating. He always has an answer for everything, yet manages to make the most ludicrous explanation sound plausible."

"You're describing *my* husband," the journalist muttered.

They both laughed.

Another reporter who hadn't cracked a smile turned to Nicco. "You were once betrothed to Princess

Benedetta. Rumor has it she never married because you broke her heart.''

Callie had been prepared to be nice, but with that reporter's unwise comment, the gauntlet had been thrown down. She was prepared to answer it for her husband.

''That's a lovely romantic notion perpetrated by members of the media who must keep the speculation going to sell papers,'' Callie interjected boldly. ''If there's any truth to the rumor, then she's to be pitied for never having had the gumption to move on with her life.''

By the indignant look in the reporter's eye, she'd angered him with her answer which had been meant for Nicco.

''So, Signora Tescotti—if it turns out the former prince were to break your heart, you, like many of your American compatriots, wouldn't have any trouble replacing him.''

''The two situations aren't comparable. Nicco *married* me. I'm his wife, whether American or Italian.'' She glanced at the man's wedding ring. ''Tonight when you get home from work, ask your wife what she would do if you left her? I believe you'll get the same answer from her you'd get from me.''

Callie eyed each of the reporters. ''Are there any more questions for me? If not, I'll defer to my husband.''

Nicco removed his arm from her shoulders and sat forward. ''We've allowed you forty-five minutes including pictures. I'll entertain one more question.''

''What did your wife give you for a wedding present?''

''Ten thousand dollars.''

The living room went quiet as the group of them blinked in surprise.

"My husband got a late start in life earning his own living. The money represented my belief in him."

"What did the former prince give you?" Evidently the hostile reporter was still smarting. He hadn't gotten the story he'd come for.

"The biggest thrill of my life. If you were a cyclist, you'd understand."

"We all remember your husband's brilliant racing career," another journalist contributed.

"That's because Nicco has a brilliant mind. One day soon people will know him for his engineering genius." She swallowed hard. "It's humbling to be the wife of such a man."

The female journalist got up first and shook Callie's hand. "Thank you for allowing us inside your home. It's obvious you and your husband are extremely happy. The very best to you."

CHAPTER TEN

"THAT was a great shoot, Mrs. Tescotti. *International Motorcycle World* will be honored to feature you on the cover. You're easy on the eyes, if you know what I mean."

Callie had just ridden up to Colin Grimes, the good-looking, thirtyish cameraman who'd flown all the way from London at Nicco's bidding. She and her Strada 100 were literally spattered by mud from riding around the Oliveras's farm while he took pictures.

Ignoring her husband who stood a few feet away from the other man who'd also raced bikes at one time she said, "Thank you, Colin. I'm the one who's honored. You work for the best cycling magazine in the business."

He winked at her. "Can I quote you on that?"

"Yes," she said, smiling into his sunny blue eyes. "I've read every magazine about sports bikes since I was ten years old. Off the record, yours is head and shoulders above the others in terms of quality stories and photography."

"Did you pay her to say this, Nicco?"

"He didn't have to," she answered for her husband who'd grown distinctly quiet over the last hour. "Now if you two will excuse me, I'd like to get back to the animal hospital. I need to clean off my bike, then shower."

Colin nodded. "We'll follow you in my rental car.

Don't forget I'm taking you to dinner before I leave for San Jose.''

"We're looking forward to it. I'll even put on a dress for the occasion. Come to think of it, my husband hasn't even seen me in a dress yet.''

Male admiration shone from his eyes. "With a wife who looks as good as you do, clothes don't matter.''

In his effort to pay her a compliment, Colin had unknowingly touched on a subject Callie had been trying in vain to forget.

"Flattery will get you everywhere, Colin Grimes,'' she teased. "I guess it's true that in the end women dress for other women.''

Still avoiding her husband's inscrutable gaze, she started up the motor. "Nicco? I'll meet you and Colin in the reception room of the clinic in an hour. I need that much time for a transformation. Hopefully neither of you will recognize me.''

Flashing them a beatific smile, she took off down the road.

A few minutes later Callie pulled around the back of the vet hospital. She grabbed the hose and cleaned her bike. After wiping it off, she put it away in the garage and entered the clinic through the back door with her medical satchel.

The second she let herself in her apartment, Ann was there to hug her.

They gravitated to the bathroom where she could lock the door.

"Thank you for pulling through for me,'' Callie whispered.

For once in her life Ann looked sheepish. "It was the

least I could do after what you were put through because of me. I guess this makes us even.''

Callie nodded. ''You look sensational in my dress.''

''We're the mirror image of each other, remember, Callie? Are you sure you want to do this? Ever since you phoned me from Locarno and told me about your plan, I've had this bad feeling.''

Her features hardened. ''You weren't there when he came close to doing the unforgivable.''

''But it didn't happen because deep down he's a good man. Look what lengths he went to for his brother.''

''That was different.''

''How?''

''Because he tricked me into saying and doing things in that guesthouse I would never ha— Oh—none of it matters anymore.''

Ann bit her lip. It was one of the mannerisms she and Callie had in common when they grew nervous or excited. ''If Nicco is as shrewd as you say he is, he's going to figure out we switched places before either of us can blink.''

Callie took a sharp breath. ''That's why I left Chloe playing with Roxy at Dr. Wood's house. As long as I have time to get away from here before that cunning brain of his computes the truth, that's all I care about. You'll need to be prepared to get out of here, too. Just as fast as you can.''

''Don't worry. I have to be on the set again day after tomorrow. Callie? Please tell me where you're going.''

''I better not or Nicco will break you down. He has a way...''

''Why don't you just admit you're in love with him and see what happens?''

"Don't you think I would if I thought he felt the same about me?" she blurted in anguish. "He had his chance in Locarno, but he didn't take it."

"I don't understand it, Callie. He sounded genuinely smitten when I talked to him from the barge."

"If it suits his purpose, he can act circles around anyone, even *you*."

Ann looked vaguely alarmed. "How long are you going to be gone?"

"I told Dr. Wood a week at the most. Any other boss would have fired me long before now. He's such a sweetie he told me my marital problems needed to be resolved first."

"In your case he's right."

"It won't be long before Nicco grows tired of this absurd game he's been playing and flies back to Italy."

"What if he doesn't?"

"Don't even think it! He can't run his business from here forever." Her anxious eyes searched Ann's. "Did you pack a bag for me?"

"Yes. I put your purse inside it. Everything's in the rental car I parked in Dr. Wood's driveway. I left it unlocked. The keys are in the ignition."

"Okay. You already know everything about Nicco, but I need to fill you in on the latest. You're going out to dinner with a very attractive man from *International Motorcycle World* named Colin Grimes. He's from London and used to race sports bikes. Now he's their head photographer.

"Nicco was in a rather foul mood when I left them at the Olivero farm, so pay more attention to him than Colin."

"It sounds like your husband's jealous."

"No," Callie said on a shaky breath. "I'm fairly certain he senses something's not right, but he can't put his finger on it."

"He sounds scary to me."

She eyed her sister solemnly. "He is… Good luck."

"Callie—"

It was the middle of the night when Callie heard a knock on the motel room door. She hadn't been asleep. The sound of waves crashing on the beach along the Big Sur had kept her awake.

If the knock hadn't been followed by her sister's voice, Callie would have phoned the desk for help.

"Callie? Wake up! Let me in."

Something terrible must have happened.

"What's wrong?" she cried in fear. Scrambling out of bed in her nightgown, she was all thumbs trying to unlock the dead bolt. "How did you know I would come here?"

She opened the door, then let out a gasp. *"Nicco!"*

"Did you really think you could get away from me?" His tall, dark frame filled the doorway. Then he was inside the room and there was nowhere for her to hide.

He nudged the door shut with his foot. In the semi-darkness he looked big and powerful, acting very much like the prince he'd once been.

She lifted her softly rounded chin in defiance. "No. I just needed some time to myself. We've lived together day and night for an entire month."

"That's what newlyweds do."

"Please, Nicco. Don't start that again." When she saw his gaze travel over her body in intimate appraisal, she sprang for her robe lying on the end of the bed.

After she'd slipped it on and tied the belt, she faced him once more. "We're on the verge of being divorced."

To her consternation he walked over to the queen-size bed and sat down on it. Still staring at her he said, "Did you file?"

"You *know* I didn't."

He shrugged those magnificent shoulders of his. "Neither did I."

"Listen here, Nicco." Her hands had tightened into fists. "You were the one who drafted that ghastly document. You led me to believe you'd taken care of everything!"

"I would have. But after being married to you for a month, I decided I didn't like the terms. I'm here to draw up new ones. Fortunately your sister decided to cooperate and led me to the place she figured you had to be. It saved me hiring a private detective."

"I should have known I couldn't trust her."

"In all fairness to her, she did her best to vamp me. Ann Lassiter is quite a woman. However I'd know my own wife anywhere and I recognized the imposter for who she was the second she waltzed into the reception room at the clinic.

"I'd have been here sooner, but I had to get rid of Colin first. He found himself charmed by the real Mrs. Tescotti, but I'm afraid it was your sister who brought the poor devil to his knees.

"When he sends me the proofs, I'll fill him in on the beautiful Lassiter twins' latest caper and end his misery. If I'm not mistaken, Ann hasn't seen the last of him."

Anger filled her cheeks with flame. "My sister has a

lot to answer for. I wasn't the one who signed the marriage contract from hell.''

''That's an apt description. My bride has never been at a loss for words. I've decided it's your greatest trait.''

''You're totally amoral, do you know that?''

''I've known it for years. Otherwise I wouldn't have turned my back on the throne.'' He was sounding bored again, increasing her fury.

''If you think I'd sign anything conceived by the master of deceit, then you don't know me at all. I grant you your freedom. Take it and go!''

''I've been thinking about what you said in Locarno.'' He went on talking as if she hadn't said a word.

''I said a lot of insane things,'' she bit out. ''How dare you remind me!''

''Did you mean it about being there for me in any capacity? About being the mother of my child?''

She hugged her arms to her waist. ''You're cruel, you know that?''

''I had a talk with Father last week while I was at the office. I promised we'd make him a 'papo' as soon as it was humanly possible. He told me Mother has already bought two christening gowns. One for Enzo and Maria's baby, and one for ours. We can't disappoint her now. Don't you want a baby we've made together?''

Callie struggled for breath. ''Someday I want several. With the right man.''

''What would I have to change about myself to be that man? I come with connections. Enzo and I had a long talk over the phone the other day after he returned from his honeymoon.

''His first official act as prince is to donate the estate with the hunting lodge where you operated on Valentino to the public. He's turning it into a national wildlife sanctuary and animal shelter.

"It's part of a vision he's had for years. All creatures great and small, homeless or unwanted, will find a home there. He's already looking for someone to oversee the whole program and keep it running smoothly. Someone with Dr. Donatti's credentials and an instinctive love for animals."

Don't say any more.

"Mother and Father are insisting that Enzo and Maria move into the palace with them; therefore the small palace on the estate will be available for the head of the foundation to live in and work. I told Enzo he need look no further than my bride."

"Enough! You turned your back on your heritage years ago. Now you expect me to believe you'd live *there*?"

"I'm not the prince. As you pointed out to those journalists who've never been the same since that interview, I leave for my own work at eight o'clock in the morning and don't get home until six at night. If it's my wife's job description to live on the estate where she works, then of course we'll make our home there. Ours is a partnership.

"You have to admit the apartment is already cramped with Valentino constantly underfoot. If you can picture it with the addition of Chloe and the children we're going to have, then your imagination is better than mine."

Nicco had gone too far. Without love on his part, everything he was saying had become pure punishment.

"Get out of here right now or I'll call the police."

He flashed her a satisfied smile. "I dare you. When

they learn we're on our honeymoon, they'll realize it's a domestic squabble and leave.''

Her brows met in a frown. ''You have honeymoon on the brain. What you need is a woman who can stand to put up with you. Why don't you arrange for a new Hollywood benefit with the real *you* offered as the grand prize?

''It would be entitled, Who Wants To Marry An Ex-Prince? Hosts of beautiful women won't be able to resist signing up as a participant. Anyone knows that an ex-prince is twice as exciting as a prince. You'll tap into the bad boy jaded royal image and find your perfect mate.''

''I'm looking at her right now. She gives as good as she gets.''

''I'm not available. Apparently Princess Benedetta still is.''

''Valentino has already bonded to you. Did you really mean it when you said I gave you the greatest thrill of your life?''

''I never say what I don't mean.''

''Were you referring to the bike I gave you for a wedding present?''

''Nicco—'' She shook her head in despair. ''When is this going to end?'' she cried with tears in her voice.

''When you tell me you love me. When I hear that you're so in love with me, you can't breathe for wanting me. When you lie in my arms like you did at the guesthouse and beg me to make love to you for the rest of our lives. How long are you going to go on torturing me?''

His question set her on fire, a fire that filled her whole

body and soul. She lifted her head, staggered by the revelation that he'd been suffering too.

"W-when did you fall in love with me?" She still couldn't take it in.

"The moment you asked me if I was one of Enzo's bodyguards. Your withering response to my answer was like an intoxicant I couldn't get enough of."

"I lost my heart to you even sooner than that," she finally confessed, unable to hold back any longer.

"It happened the second you caught me staring at you in the airport lounge. Oh, Nicco. You were the most exciting man I'd ever seen in my life. I fell for you on the spot and love you so terribly, you can't imagine. The pain of having to hold back my feelings has almost destroyed me."

"Don't ever hold them back again, Callie," he whispered in an aching voice. "I need you too much. Come over here, darling, so we can end the pain and really start to live."

She didn't remember touching the floor. His strong arms reached for her and then their mouths and bodies began to move as one flesh. She'd thought riding on the back of his bike where their bodies seemed to meld together had been ecstasy...

EPILOGUE

"I BAPTIZE this infant Anna Lassiter Tescotti, in the name of the Father, the Son and the Holy Ghost. Amen."

Father Luigi passed their perfectly behaved baby girl back to Nicco whose happiness seemed to have taken ten years off him. It gave her a glimpse of the younger Nicco, but she was thankful she hadn't met him when his tortured soul held him in its grip.

The time hadn't been right for either of them.

Callie's gaze drifted back to Anna with her cap of glossy black curls and cherub face. She had tiny black eyelashes that brought attention to her deep-set eyes. It looked like they were going to be green. Her determined chin was exactly like Nicco's.

He was crazy about her. So was her papo.

Poor Valentino. He'd never had competition before. It was a good thing Chloe was out of quarantine and had moved into the palace with them at last. The boxer didn't know what to make of her, but she'd definitely provided a needed distraction for him.

For some reason, Chloe seemed to respond to that indifference and had been following him around, not only inside the palace, but out on the estate. It was very strange considering the pug was really a house dog and afraid of her own shadow.

Chloe kind of reminded Callie of herself. Nicco's

splendid indifference to her at the airport had changed the course of her life forever.

She lifted her shimmering green gaze to her husband once more and found him smiling at her. It wasn't like any other smile he'd ever given her.

This one held such sweetness, she knew that every lingering shadow in his heart had fled.

How come I'm so blessed, she mouthed the words to him.

Father Luigi chose that moment to clear his throat. "Nicco? In as much as you wish to renew your wedding vows, if you'll relinquish your daughter to one of the family, we'll proceed."

To Callie's astonishment, instead of making a beeline for his mother, he carried their daughter to her aunt Ann who was standing next to Colin. As he transferred their precious child to her arms, she saw Nicco's lips move. He was thanking her sister for bringing them together.

Callie had already thanked Ann a thousand times. She'd probably go on thanking her forever, especially since her sister was going to take care of their baby and the dogs while she and Nicco went on a short honeymoon.

Nicco finally turned to Callie and grasped her hand. After kissing the palm, he drew her in front of the priest who looked especially pleased.

"Dearly Beloved, let us begin. Do you, Callie Ann Lassiter Tescotti, take Nicco Tescotti for your cherished husband?"

She turned to Nicco. "I did the first time, darling, and do so again. I love you with all my heart and soul." Her tremulous voice reached the furthermost regions of the chapel.

"Nicco? Do you take Callie Ann for your espoused wife to honor and adore until death do you part?"

Never taking his eyes off of Callie he answered solemnly, "Of course. She's my life." His voice had gone gruff with emotion.

Callie could hear a lot of sniffing behind her. Maria was still as emotional as Callie. Their little boy, Prince Alberto the Second, named after Nicco's father, had dimples and looked just like Enzo who appeared to be the happiest of men.

This sacred moment had reduced the proud grandparents of two new Tescotti offspring to tears as well. Maria's parents, Dr. Wood and the Donattis stood next to them beaming with pride.

"You may kiss your bride, Nicco."

Her husband immediately cupped Callie's face in his hands. "Are you ready for our ride?" he whispered. His black eyes gleamed with rakish excitement. When Nicco looked like that, he blinded her with his male beauty.

"I've been living for it," she whispered back.

"I'm glad you said that. Frankly I can't wait to get out of our wedding clothes."

Callie murmured, "I was thinking the same thing."

On that note he kissed her long and hard. When he finally allowed her to breathe he said, "Thank God you love me. I'd already named your new motorcycle *The Princess Bride* when I submitted the magazine article for publication."

She frowned. "You're kidding—aren't you? Dare I ask your other choice?"

His face darkened with lines. *"The Runaway Bride."*

"Nicco—you don't give motorcycles such ridiculous names—"

After an elegant shrug, he burst into the kind of rich laughter she loved so much.

"Ooh, I'm going to get you for that."

"Why do you think I said it?" He kissed the end of her well-shaped nose. "Life with you is one huge adventure. I never want it to end."

"Neither do I, darling."

Their mouths fused in passion once more.

Neither do I.